The Last Real Nigga Alive

A Novel by Tranay Adams

The Last Real Nigga Alive

The Last Real Nigga Alive / Tranay Adams-1st ed.© 2016

Formatting: Renee Lamb

Editor: Ghost

Cover Artist: Sunny Giovanni

Publisher: Tranay Adams

Chapter 1

"This nigga is willing to pay fifty a brick? Are you sure this cat isn't a fed?" Carlo asked King from the front passenger seat, where he pressed the red safety button on and off on his Beretta. He wore a Sacramento Kings snapback and a matching jersey.

"Nah, this nigga not one of the alphabet boys," King said from behind the wheel. He wore a pair of designer shades with maroon lenses, a wife-beater and tan cargo shorts.

"You sure?" Carlo asked for reassurance, "Nigga willing to pay fifty a bird…smells fishy to me. He gotta be one of them people to let chu beat'em over the head like that." That nigga Carlo shook his head disbelievingly. He was looking to get off the blocks that they were sitting on, but the ticket price these fools were looking to buy them for sounded too good to be true for him.

"Nah, this nigga from outta town, he's from New Orleans. It's a drought out there." King told him. He didn't know this new cat from a hole in the wall. In fact, he'd just met him at some dump over on the eastside called The Bar Fly. The dude got to talking about how he was looking for a new plug because he was getting hit over the head back home with prices. Niggaz had kilos going for sixty, but he wasn't trying to lay down that kind of gwap for a brick. So he took a drive out to California hoping to find someone that could set him straight with some decent work at a cool price. When King gave the cat the quote for fifty a bird, he jumped at it. The cat said he needed ten of those "bitches" ASAP. Hearing that was like music to King's ears. All he could see were dollar signs before his eyes. He didn't waste any time shooting to his stash spot to get his birds.

"You sure about this fool, King, man?" he looked to his homeboy for reassurance. That small voice at the back of his head was screaming at him 'Naw, nigga, fallback' but the hustler in him was screaming back, *'Nigga, you betta get this money.'* He was indecisive, so he needed his right-hand man to sway his decision.

"Positive." He glanced from the windshield to his main man, as he drove through the streets. He gave him the reassuring look that he needed and nodded. That was all his nigga needed.

"Alright, let's get it."

"Let's get it." He took one of his hands from off of the wheel and dapped him up. "My nigga," He chuckled and smiled.

***

"Say, bruh, how'd you come across this nigguh here?" Cortez asked Mar'vel in a New Orleans drawl as he casually sipped on Hennessy over the rocks, licking his big ass lips. He was a skinny cinnamon complexioned nigga with short dark brown dreadlocks and a cross tattooed between his eyes. This mothafucka looked like a knock off Lil' Wayne.

"I saw homie at the bar I was chillin' at," Mar'vel answered, glancing at his Rolex trying to see if it was time for his plug to arrive yet. "He looked like a get-money type a nigguh, so I hollered at'em on some ol' small talk shit, ya know? At some point or another we started talkin' 'bout hustlin' and I told'em it was a drought where I was from. Nigguh started boastin' 'bout how he's doin' it big out here and how he got unlimited keys and shit; straight stuntin'. Said he lettin'em go for fiddy a piece. I told'em I wanted ten of dem bitches, ya heard me? Now here we are."

"Nigguh, bit da bait, huh? Ol' greedy muddafucka, he gone learn today, though," Cortez said, picking up his semi-automatic handgun and checking the magazine in it. Once he saw that it was fully loaded, he smacked it back in and cocked it.

CLICK! CLACK!

"Fiddy bands a square?" Mar'vel shook his head, like it didn't make no goddamn sense. "Dem fed prices, muddafucka so money hungry he didn't even stop to think that he maybe dealin' wit dem people, or headed for a double cross. These Cali niggaz prolly think we're just some dumb country bwois. That's okay, 'cause we 'bouta put these bitches in a blender." He was a baby face dude with a Lil' Boosie fade.

KNOCK! KNOCK! KNOCK!

"That's dem, Bruh, get into position," he told his main man before tucking his banger into the small of his back and heading for the door. Mar'vel unlocked and unchained the raggedy door before snatching it open. "What's happenin', bruh?" he slapped hands with King.

"What that shit do, my nigga?" King replied.

"Who dis?" A frowning Mar'vel asked him.

"This is my brotha, Carlo." King answered, looking from his man to his brother.

"What's up, lil daddy?" Mar'vel raised his calloused hand to greet Carlo.

Carlo looked at homie's hand as if it were dripping wet with piss and then asked, "You the feds, Homie?" he inquired with a hard-face.

Mar'vel laughed and looked to that nigga King. "Is this nigguh serious?" he asked with a chuckle. King shrugged. "Nah, I ain't no muddafuckin' fed, I'ma bitness man, play bwoi!"

Carlo brushed past Mar'vel into the motel room. He checked the lamps and telephone for bugs, but couldn't find anything.

"You satisfied? Can we get to bitness now?" Mar'vel asked him.

King looked to his little brother and he nodded.

"Where the paper at?" King asked Mar'vel.

"I got it nearby." Mar'vel said. "Let me test out one of dem bricks, though." King nodded. He unzipped the duffle bag and pulled out a brick, handing it over to him. Mar'vel hacked off a chunk of the brick and dropped it into a boiling Pyrex pot of water. The chunk of cocaine bubbled in the liquid and succumbed to a harder form. It was now a crack rock. He smiled like the cat that swallowed the canary. The chunk conforming to a solid rock so quickly meant that the cocaine was pure. He could come up off the work that King had on deck.

"You fucking with me or what, baby? Let a nigga know something."King smiled, looking at him like he knew he had the best cocaine in the world.

"I want all ten of dem bitches." Mar'vel smiled, boasting a grill filled with shiny gold teeth. "Ya heard me? All ten," He said louder.

That was Cortez's signal; he sprung up from the side of the bed like a Jack in the Box, wearing a T-shirt over his head. All that could be seen were his terrifying eyes through the neck-hole as he pointed the AK-47 between King and Carlo. "Drop it like it's hot, nigguh! Lay that shit down, ya bitch!" he barked. Carlo cursed himself for falling for the set-up as he pulled the banger from his waistline and laid it down at his feet. Mar'vel, who had his banger pressed against the side of his dome, snarled at him. Cortez kept his choppa trained on King and his brother as he approached them with a roll of duct-tape. He handed it to King and told him to tape Carlo's wrists and ankles together. Once King did like he was told, Mar'vel tucked his banger and taped his wrists and ankles with the duct-tape. After he was done he checked the duffle bag and found a total of nine blocks of cocaine wrapped in cellophane.

"They're all here." Mar'vel said before zipping up the duffle bag and slinging it over his shoulder. "Toss me that pillow, nigga!" he told Cortez. Cortez tossed him a pillow off of the bed. He caught it in the air and placed it to the back of Carlo's head as he struggled to get free. He then pressed his banger in behind it and squeezed off twice, halting Carlo's movements. He then placed the pillow to the back of King's head and pressed his banger in behind it, pulling the trigger two more times. He pulled the banger away and the barrel wafted with smoke.

King and his sibling lie on the flat carpet stiff, their life's blood expanding over the floor. Mar'vel pulled a camouflage bandana from his back pocket and tossed it to Cortez, telling him to wipe everything down that he'd touched, while he did the same with an identical bandana.

"It's checkout time, play bwoi." Mar'vel told his homeboy.

BOOM!

The door flew open sending splinters flying everywhere. Two DEA agents, a hulking man and a slim woman, dressed in caps and windbreakers with DEA emblazoned across the back of them, dropped the battering-ram they'd used to bust the door open. The woman raised her Desert Eagle; while the big man raised his chrome .44 Magnum revolver and his black .357 Magnum revolver.

"Move and your shits in the wind!" the hulking man bellowed.

"Drop'em mothafuckaz!" the slim woman barked. "Drop'em or I'll drop your asses!"

Hesitantly, Cortez and Mar'vel laid down their weapons. They got down on their knees with their hands behind their heads as one of the DEA agents had ordered them.

"We got'em," The hulking man spoke into his walkie-talkie. He then placed the walkie-talkie back on his waistline and he and his partner handcuffed them, making them lay flat on their stomachs. He stashed his revolvers into their respective holsters and turned to his partner. "Nice going, Ironhorn!" he high fived the slim woman.

"Thanks, Pivens." The slim woman replied. She unzipped the duffle bag and saw the ten blocks of cocaine inside. The sight brought a smile to her face, "Ten joints." Pivens whistled hearing how many blocks of cocaine were stuffed inside of the duffle bag. "Let's see what these dead mothafuckaz got on'em, check these two out." He nodded to Mar'vel and Cortez. Pivens recovered a few bands from King and Carlo's bodies, while Ironhorn came up with a few from Mar'vel and Cortez.

"It's gotta be more loot than this here." Pivens said to Ironhorn. He stepped to Mar'vel and nudged him with his boot, "My man, where the paper at?" While Pivens was talking, Mar'vel was staring at the ski-mask tattooed on his neck and the inscription surrounding it: Get Rich or Die Broke. "Do you hear me talking to you?"

"There ain't no muddafuckin' paper, nigguh." Mar'vel spat. "Oof!" Pivens kicked him in the side, cracking his ribs. His face twisted in agony and he blinked as if his eyes were being attacked by fluorescent lights. "Bullshit! Now your swamp feet, gator wrestling ass gone tell me where the money is," Piven's spat, gripping the handle of his long nose .357 Magnum revolver tighter. "Or its hammer time." He pressed his sneaker to the side of Mar'vel's head and pushed the black steel into his temple.

"Fuck you!" Mar'vel barked. "Tez these niggaz ain't po-po! They're some mudda-fuckin' jack boys!"

"What the fuck!" Cortez cursed. "How da fuck y'all gone jack us for da shit we jacked?"

"Easy," Ironhorn said, putting her sneaker on Cortez's back and pointing the same AK-47 he had earlier at the back of his dome. "It's a cold world, my nigga, you best grab a jacket."

"Fuck y'all bitches, man! Fuck y'all, suck my dick! I'ma gangsta, I ain't scared to die!" Spittle flew from Mar'vel's lips.

"I feel you, now feel this!" Pivens scowled and snarled.

BOOM! BOOM! BOOM! BOOM!

The thunderous roars of the cannon bounced off the motel room's walls. Moments later, Zay and La'Chat hurried out of the motel room ten bricks richer.

MEAN WHILE IN THE MOTEL LOBBY

The telephone rang until the answering machine picked it up.

"Hello, this is the Majesty Motel; sorry we weren't in to answer your call, but please feel free to leave a message. Otherwise, listen to our rates and specials..." the voice, which obviously belonged to a Middle Eastern clerk, went on to give the rates and specials.

The Arabian clerk and his wife lie on their stomachs with their wrists and ankles duct-taped together. There was a gaping hole at the back of his head and his white turban was now red. The back of his wife's head was blown out and horror was etched upon their faces.

Chapter 2

"Oooooh, shit!" Montrice wailed as the pelvis of an ebony form crashed into her middle. Her thick legs were pinned above her head as he worked her pussy, sliding his dick in and out of it. The ebony man shined from perspiration, his back muscles flexing. Sweat dripped from his brow as he handled his business. His face mirrored the intensity and pleasure he embodied. Veins formed in his forehead and neck. The muscles in his arms and calves shown from the intensity he was expelling. He breathed heavily, chest jumping up and down.

"Haa! Haa! Haa! Haa!" He pounded away, the headboard of the bed banging up against the wall.

"Fuck me! Fuck me, nigga! Deeper! Deeper! Yes, Oh, God! I feel it! I feel it!" the louder Montrice cried, the harder he laid into her; just like she liked it: rough and nasty. Montrice's eyes bugged and rolled into the back of her head, mouth dropping open. Her cries of passion had turned into a shriek, her legs going into convulsions. The ebony man stopped in mid pump and looked down, sweat dripping from his forehead every couple of seconds. He was waiting for something, and he got it.

"Ooooooh, fuuuck," Montrice pressed her head further back into the pillow and her mouth stretched wide open, her tongue vibrating as she shrilled. Her back rose up from off of the mattress. Clenching the sheets in her hands, her body jerked and she sprayed the sheets with her love nectar. Once she'd gotten hers off, she collapsed onto the bed. Her succulent breasts rose and fell, with each breath that she took, breathing hard from her orgasm. Seeing that his fuck-buddy was pleased, the ebony man started up again. His wet flesh smacked up against hers and the veins in his grown man became more visible. Feeling the semen building up in his member, he started grinding harder into her. His eyes narrowed into slits and his mouth quivered. His eyes rolled to their whites, looking like Q-balls were inside of his head.

"Mmmmmmmmm," She squeezed her eyes shut and bit down hard on her bottom lip, her French tip toes up in the air. The headboard banged up against the wall harder and faster, as her sex partner worked feverishly towards unleashing seeds that had stirred awake in his souther region. His dickhead pulsated, and his pee hole seemed to expand and shrink. Suddenly, he grunted and erupted, oozing his hot semen deep inside of her womb. He collapsed on the side of her, chest inflating and deflating as he breathed.

"Damn, Lafayette, you've got some bomb ass dick. Haa! Haa! Haa! Haa," Montrice feasted her hazel green eyes on her fuck-buddy's glistening, semi-erect dick as she stroked it up and down. It looked like a baseball bat dipped in chocolate. She grinned, watching clear fluid run from out of its hole, sliding over her knuckles.

"So, I've been told." Lafayette smiled arrogantly, staring up at the ceiling with his hands clasped behind his head. He knew he had a platinum dick and a golden tongue. His head had ballooned with all of the compliments he'd received from his sex partners over the years.

"Don't get cocky, nigga." Montrice chuckled and playfully punched him in the shoulder. She then quickly pecked him on the lips and laid the side of her face against his chest, caressing his peck with her hand.

Lafayette picked up a wrinkled pack of Newport 100s from off of the dresser. He pulled out a cigarette with his lips and picked up a book of matches. He tore out one of the sticks and swiped it across the black strip on the back of it.

Shhhhhh!

The flame sounded as a reddish orange flame was born. Lafayette put the fire to the end of the cancer stick and took a couple of puffs, expelling white smoke. He fanned out the flame and tossed the burnt out match into the waste basket by the bed.

Montrice looked at the digital clock on the dresser. It was 8: 35 A.M. Her eyes bulged and her eyebrows rose, her head shooting up from off of Lafayette's chest. "Shit. I gotta get back on the clock, let me take a shower." She jumped out of bed swiftly.

Lafayette took the square from his lips and looked to Montrice, blowing smoke out towards the ceiling. He watched as she hurried into the bathroom, her big red buttocks jiggling with each step she took. Through the cracked open door of the bathroom, Lafayette observed her wetting a washcloth beneath the flowing faucet and used it to wipe off the semen that had oozed from out of her pussy and down her legs. Montrice wringed out the washcloth and set it aside, turned on the shower. The showerhead sprayed hot water that quickly began to fill the bathroom up with steam. Montrice kissed her palm and blew a kiss at Lafayette. He caught it and placed it over his heart, with a smirk. She then closed the bathroom door to take her shower.

Lafayette reached over the side of the bed and picked up the top to Montrice's black work uniform. He looked at her nameplate which bared her last name "Shakur". Using the hand that he held the cigarette with, he caressed the city within the police shield. A line etched across his forehead, he was literally sleeping with the enemy. He was a drug dealer. She was an officer of the law. It was her job to take criminals like him down. And it was his job to never get caught.

Lafayette sat up in bed and slipped on his boxer-briefs. He pushed his nightstand forward and pulled a camcorder free from behind its glass mirror. He rewound the footage and watched a little of him and Montrice's sexual escapade. A smile emerged on his face. Lafayette took a copper key from his top dresser drawer and carried his 5 foot 10 frame over to the closet. He unlocked the door and placed the camcorder on the top shelf along with a massive collection of video cassette tapes of all of his sexual rumps. The nigga had a thing for filming himself. He liked watching himself in action, running dick up in all kinds of women. Sometimes when he was bored he'd pop some popcorn and watch one of his tapes. His collection spanned way back to when he was in high school, knocking down his fourth period English teacher, Ms. Harvey.

Lafayette closed the closet door and locked it back. He went to drop the copper key into his top dresser drawer when he heard an eerie noise. He looked to Montrice's purse and saw a light flashing inside of it. It dawned on him that it had to have been her cell phone. Curiosity got the best of him and he dipped his hand into the designer bag, producing her cellular. A name was on the screen in bold letters: HUBBY. He smiled wickedly and read the text message.

HOW ABOUT LUNCH AT BERTHA'S TODAY?

Lafayette decided to answer back, tapping the letters on the screen.

I'LL TAKE A RAINCHECK, I'M STILL FULL FROM EATIN YOUR WIFEY'S PUSSY LMAO #COLDWORLD

Lafayette laughed to himself and deleted the message. He wasn't about to text Montrice's husband and fuck up a happy home. Women played games like that. He was too much of a player to stoop to that level. He respected the game

Hearing the dials being turned off and the shower water shutting off, Lafayette dropped the device back into the purse and lay back in the bed, smoking his Joe.

FIVE MINUTES LATER

Lafayette walked Montrice out of the back door of his house, feasting his eyes on her curvaceous form in her tight fitting black police officers' uniform along the way. He admired the sway of her big old ass as she threw it from left to right. Her movements made her buttocks appear as if they were doing a dance.

"Damn, boo, look at them meat hooks, um uh," Lafayette bit down on his bottom lip. Montrice stopped and gave him a little shake before walking forth, chuckling. He unlocked the back gate and rolled it back. He snatched open the driver side door of her police cruiser and she hopped in behind the wheel. He slammed the door shut behind her and leaned over inside of the window, resting his arms on the pane.

Montrice fired up the engine and turned to him, showcasing all thirty-two of her beautiful white teeth.

"So, am I going to see you tonight?" she asked, dimples in her cheeks.

"Sorry, Boo, I can't play tonight. I got some shit I gotta do. Besides, we wouldn't want hubby getting suspicious."

Montrice sucked her teeth and waved him off. "Please, he needs to be happy that I'm still letting him taste this pussy, with his sorry ass. Don't get me wrong, he's a good guy and all. He's even OK in the sack, but sometimes I wanna be fucked, not made love to, feel me?"

Man, no matter what you do for these bitches it's never enough. They always want more. Here this bitch is married to a cat that's done gave her everything that she could dream of and she still isn't satisfied. These hoes ain't shit. That's why I'ma stay single and baby momma free, Lafayette thought as he smiled and nodded to what he'd just been told.

"Aye, if he was taking care of business, then I'd be outta business." Lafayette capped.

"Sho' ya right." Montrice leaned her head out of the window and locked lips with him, slipping him a little tongue. She wiped her mouth with the back of her hand and said, "Call me, OK?" he nodded and she took off down the alley, jumping behind the wheel of her cruiser. The gravel crunched under the pressure of her vehicle tires.

Chapter 3

KNOCK! KNOCK! KNOCK! KNOCK!

Gar had been knocking on his baby momma's apartment door for the past five minutes, but no one had arrived to open it. He was growing agitated by the minute. It was early in the morning and cool outside so he was eager to get inside where it was warm. He had a key to the place but he'd lost it a few days ago. He was so busy running the streets that he hadn't gotten another one made. He wasn't really worried about it because his baby momma was home most of the time anyway.

"It's as cold as a pimp's heart out here." Gar rubbed his hands together trying to keep warm, shoulders hunched. He tried peering through the window but he couldn't see anything due to the glass being smudged with dirt. "I know this bitch hear me knocking on this mothafucking door." He scowled and ran his hands up and down his arms, still trying to peer through the filthy window. He rapped on the door once again and then yelled out, "Batice, open the fucking door, I know you hear me out here!" His white breath appeared in the cool air.

Gar quieted down once he saw a silhouette move past the window and heard the locks being undid. The front door was snatched open. A pale skinned chick with gold dookie braids and baby blue eyes stood before him. Her face was screwed up and she had her hand on her hip, weight leaning to one side. She was in a black halter top and Daisy Dukes with the pockets hanging out the bottoms of them. The shorts were unbuttoned at the top so her panties were exposed. Batice was an OK looking girl, but the acne scars on her cheeks made her a four on the scale at best. She had a pinch of breasts and little shape to speak of, but the junk in her trunk brought its fair share of attention. It had every nigga in the hood trying run dick up in her, and a fair share of cats got to. It didn't take much to get Batice in the mood. A bottle of that Hen Dog and a Ziploc of that good and she was with whatever.

"Damn, Gar, you're knocking on the door like you're Binem!" Batice spat with a hint of attitude, moving her neck like the hoodrat that she was and combing her fingers through her individual braids. She shifted the weight of her body to her opposite leg and placed her hand on her hip. "What chu won't?"

"Fuck you mean, what do I want?" Gar's eyebrows arched and his nose srunched up, clenching his jaws. "Bitch, I live here! Fuck take you so long to open the door?"

"I was asleep." She lied. "Why didn't you get chu another key made?" she scratched between her braids and patted them, real ghetto like and rolled her eyes. She was annoyed by him.

"Don't question me. I pay all the rent and all the bills up in this mothafucka. I'm the king of this here castle, so when I knock you come running. You got that?" He stepped closer to her, breathing fire, nostrils pulsating.

"Whatever, Clarence, if you're the king of this here castle…Start bringing your black ass home then. I get lonely sometimes. Shit, a bitch has needs."

"Like I told you before, I'm out here tryna get it." He emphasized, smacking the back of his hand into his palm heatedly. "And it's not gonna happen for me laying up in bed with cho trifling ass. If I gotta be up all day and night grinding, then so be it. Fuck sleep, I'll catch some Z's when I'm dead." Something on Batice's halter top caught Gar's eye. He pinched the end of her halter and pulled it toward him, narrowing his eyes. There was dry semen on her top. His face twisted into a mask of rage and he locked his jaws, showcasing the bone structure in his face.

"What?" Batice asked innocently. She looked down at the stain and her eyes bugged, mouth dropping open, "Oh, my God!"

"You trifling whore!" Spit flew off of his lips.

"Bae, it's not what chu think." She placed a hand to his chest, as his spit clung to her face.

"The fuck it ain't," he smacked her hand down and whipped out his .45 automatic handgun. "That nigga still in the house?" The nigga didn't give her a chance to reply. He shoved her little ass aside and stormed through the door over the threshold. He ran straight for the bedroom, murder on his brain. Nearing the doorway of the bedroom, he could see a young man in a light grey Dickie button up shirt, opened to his wife-beater and matching pants climbing out of the window. "Mothafucka," Gar bellowed, stealing the young man's attention. When the nigga looked up at Gar he was raising his .45, finger attempting to curl around the trigger. He shut his left eye and pulled the trigger as Batice jumped on his back, knocking off his aim. The bullet went wild. It missed its intended target and shattered the glass window the young nigga was climbing out of.

"No! Don't kill'em!" Batice shouted, trying to knock the banger free from her man's hand.

"Bitch, get off of me!" Gar spun around in circles with her clinging to his back for dear life. He slammed himself up against the hallway wall, causing her to bump her head. Dazed, she let go of him and hit the carpet on her side, wincing. When Gar turned around he saw homie in the Dickie shirt climbing out of the bedroom window. Once he jumped out, he took note of the neighbor's dogs barking, and that's when he knew that he was running back to the front of the complex. By this time he could hear his baby boy crying but he ignored him. As far as he was concerned, the little nigga could wait because he had more pressing matters to attend to, like running that nigga down that was fucking his baby momma.

Gar turned around and ran back towards the front door, passing a dizzy Batice. The girl was slowly climbing the wall to her feet, trying desperately to shake off the birds and stars that were circling her head. She hadn't even taken notice of her baby's daddy, who was now climbing the black guard rail outside. On bending knees and gripping the rail, he looked down below and spotted the nigga his baby momma was smashing hauling ass. Quickly, Gar tucked his .45 on his waistline and counted to himself, timing his jump. When he reached the last number on the countdown, he leaped off of the rail. His clothing ruffled as he plummeted towards the surface, closing the distance between him and homie he was hunting, fast.

"Ooof," Gar landed on his back and he staggered forward, crashing to the ground. When the young nigga's face met with the asphalt, there was a sickening crack that sounded like a slab of ribs hitting the surface. Gar grabbed homeboy by his unkempt afro and peeled his face up from the ground. Blood came rushing from out of his nostrils and mouth. He could taste metal in his grill. The mothafucka'z eyes were rolled to their whites and he was moaning in pain. His nose was broken and his front teeth were missing. His mouth was red and his loose teeth were on the surface below him, burgundy splotches littering the ground.

"You done stuck your dick in the wrong nigga'z bitch!" Gar said, looking as if a demonic spirit had possessed him. Wrinkles formed around the beginning of his nose and his eyes twinkled with murder in them. Swiftly, he snatched his .45 from his waistline and pressed it to the back of the young nigga's neck, "Lights out, Homeboy."

"Gar, nooooooo," Batice cried, hurrying down the steps with their eight month old son on her hip. Her eyes were red and her face was slicked wet. The baby's cheeks were also wet and his lip was pouty. Gar looked up at his son and he was reaching out to him. He looked between his son and the mothafucka beneath him. He then exhaled and rose to his feet, tucking his gun back in his Levi's 501 jeans. He stepped over his prey and took his offspring into his arms, kissing him on the cheek.

"Hey, man, how are you doing today?" he bounced his prince up and down. He tickled his chin and made him smile, exposing the few teeth that had grown. Niggas would have been looking at Gar like he was bat shit crazy, seeing him going from lunatic to daddy so fast. "You missed your daddy, huh? You miss your old man?" the baby laughed.

Gar stepped closer to Batice, staring her dead in the eyes and clenching his jaws. "If I ever see you with that mothafucka again, I'ma leave you both where ever the fuck I find you. Do I make myself clear?" he asked, pointing a finger in her face. She nodded her head fast and wiped her eyes, with a curled finger, sniffling.

"What the fuck, man, you straight?" Lafayette approached, with his Death Dealer out, the sun kissed off of the side of the metal gun. He looked from the hurt young man, then back up to Gar. The sun was at his back giving him an eerie glow, with his upper half being covered by the shade. No one could make out his face under the intense rays of the sun, but they all knew who he was.

"I got my son for the day." Gar told Batice, hoping that she bucked so he could kick her ass. "When I get back to the house I want some chicken tacos ready and waiting."

"All right," Batice nodded. She went to kiss him, but he turned his face away from her.

"Don't try to kiss me; probably done had this nigga's dick all down your mothafucking throat." He shook his head pitifully. This wasn't the first time he'd caught her cheating. In fact, it was the third. The two niggas before the mothafucka in the Dickie shirt were left dead, thanks to his .45. He would have surely killed homie he caught up in his bitch today had it not been for him seeing his little man. It was something about having a son that had slowed him down. Now, don't get it fucked up. The niggas was a straight up killer that would bust your head to the skull bone, but these days he was particular about the risks that he took.

Gar spared the young man a second glance and kicked him in the ribs, causing him to howl in pain. He then looked to his brother from another. "Come on, La, we're up."

"What happened back there?" Lafayette asked once they'd cleared the yard, walking down the street. He'd just tuck his heat on his waistline.

Gar looked over his shoulder and saw Batice helping old boy to his feet.

"Caught Batice fucking around," Gar shook his head sadly.

"Again?" Lafayette's brows furrowed, looking like 'Goddamn, that bitch always fucking somebody'. "Man, Batice ain't nothing but a gutta snipe ho. I don't know why you don't quit fucking with that skeeza."

"Watch your mouth, nigga, that's my baby's motha you're talking about." Gar snapped, eyebrows arched, "Yeah, I know that she ain't shit, but I still love her, feel me? We've been together since junior high school and shit."

"My fault, you know a nigga don't mean no disrespect, it's just that…"

"I'm already knowing, homie. You aint gotta say shit. I chose to keep laying up with her sorry ass, so I just gotta deal with it. I'm just trying to give my little nigga what I've never had…a family. You know what I'm saying?" he looked to him and he nodded. "Anyway, I seen One Time roll through your spot this A.M. What's up with that?" Gar inquired, "Had me thinking you were a rat and shit. I had thought about shooting over there and dusting you off." He chuckled. Had he ever suspected that his man was a cheese eating, four legged rodent, he wouldn't hesistate to put something hot in his noodle.

"Never, I stick to the G-code. That's just my lil' police bitch I busted a couple of months ago." Lafayette told him. "You know how I do. I dicked her down good and sent her on her way. We don't love these hoes. Well, you do." He smiled.

"All right, now, don't make me raise that thumper." Gar referred to his banger, patting his waistline. He switched arms with little Gar as he rounded the corner, a Metro bus passing them by.

"What's popping with Lil Man?"

"I left him over there working the block. I was just shooting to the house to kick it with junior for a minute, but then that situation came up."

"Well, let's go by there, I wanna see how the young nigga moving."

"All right, bet."

Chapter 4

Lil Man stood on the side of the liquor store wearing a black du-rag which was beneath the hood of a black Nike sweatshirt. His Levis sagged slightly off of his ass and lie over black Cortez'. Lil Man was a brown skinned dude that didn't stand a hair over five foot five. Though he was a little guy, he had the fierceness of a lion and balls the size of an elephant.

The crackheads were standing on line as if they were waiting to purchase concert tickets. As each one approached the pint sized hustler they either held up how many rocks they wanted with their fingers or told him. Lil Man kept a close watch on the block with each crack head he served. Once he was sure The Boys in Blue weren't in sight, he dipped his hand into the pocket of his jeans for the tan rocks to give the fiends their breakfast. No sooner than he had served the last smoker, he clocked Lafayette and Gar coming from around the corner.

"What's up, my nigga? How we looking?" Lafayette inquired, slapping hands with the little nigga.

"Lovely," Lil Man answered with a smile, boasting a couple of teeth so rotten that they looked bluish black. "I gotta 'bout ten more rocks. Here," he dipped into his pocket and pulled out a wad of money, which he passed to the head nigga of the operation.

Lafayette glanced at the wad and then stuffed it into his boxers, looking around to see if anyone was watching them. "In a minute I'ma go back around the corner and get some more work."

"Bet," Lil Man said. He turned to Gar. "I see you got your mini me out here early. What's up, Lil Gar? What it do?" he said to the baby. "Lil dude looks just like you, I feel sorry for'em. He ain't gone get no pussy when he grow up."

"What?" Gar switched arms with his son and threw playful jabs at Lil Man with his freehand, and he threw a couple back. These niggas had known one another since they were sixteen and thirteen years old.

FLASHBACK

Gar met Lil Man when he was locked up in Juvenile hall. He was locked up on an armed robbery charge while Lil Man was up there on aggravated assault. He'd just so happen to enter the shower room where he found two kids standing up smiling as their picture was being taken. At their feet was Lil Man with a belt around his neck, which was being held like a leash by one of the kids. The youth's face was swollen and bloody. His left eye was fat and discolored and his lips were as big as hotlinks. There were also speckles of blood around the collar of his torn undershirt. When Gar poked his head inside of the shower room and saw what was going on, he ducked off and came back with a lock in a sock, twisting it up at either end. Afterwards, he wrapped his hand up in half of it and prepared to do battle if need be.

"Yo, cuz, take a flick wit me wit 'em like dis and send it to da homies." The shortest of the three kids said, smiling devilishly. He had a big ass head and a wide nose, his face was covered in bumps and white heads. He had a very serious acne problem. Having given the order on what he wanted done, he gripped the homemade leash and squatted over Lil Man, like those breeder niggaz do in those dog magazines, smiling. After he had taken his picture, his comrade, the taller kid who had cornrows, squatted beside Lil Man and threw up his hood, mad dogging the fool that was snapping pictures with the contraband cell phone. Flashes of white light exploded one after another and then came the sound of rumbling thunder and lightning.

Gar appeared as a blur, seemingly coming out of nowhere, swinging the weapon of his choice. It came across the shortest of the hoodlums' jaws, breaking that mothafucka. The hoodlum grimaced as he fell back, broken tooth flying and blood splattering against the wall. Before he met with the floor, Gar was cracking the other nigga upside the skull with the sock. The nigga's head deflected off of the wall and he fell to his hands and knees. He was at his attacker's mercy, and he took full advantage of it. Gar slung the sock against that bitch ass nigga's head and back, trying to break every bone in his body. The cock sucka hollered out, but that nigga Gar kept on going. Gritting, he slung that sock with all of his might sending specks of blood flying everywhere. Seeing his homie getting that work, the hoodlum hooding the cell phone jumped into the action. Having seen him about to attack the young man that had just saved him, Lil Man pounced on him like a lion. The weight of his tiny frame sent him slamming down hard on the floor, grimacing. He lay there in a daze as Lil Man punched him fast and hard in his exposed face, breaking bone and teeth. Tears flew out of the little nigga's eyes as he pummeled his abuser, spots of blood appearing on his chest and arms. He attacked the youth like a feral cat, madness in his eyes. Gripping him by the sides of his head, he peeled his lips back in a sneer and showed his teeth. Driving his head forward, he sunk his choppers into the hoodlum's cheek and bit down as hard as he could. Pulling back, he left the skeletal structure of the bone and teeth in his face. The young man's pupils seem to dilate as he screamed bloody murder, his voice echoing off of the walls inside of the restroom. Lil Man stared down at his prey, chest heaving. The chunk of flesh was still in his mouth as he observed his handiwork, dripping blood to the floor. Gar cringed as he watched the little dude spit the chunk off to the side, seeing it slide across the surface. He then rose to his feet and wiped his bloody chin off with the back of his fist, still focused on the son of a bitch that had beaten the living shit out of him. He listened to his whimpering for a time before proceeding to kick and stomp him.

"Old bitch ass niggaz, couldn't fade a lil' young nigga by himself, you hoes had to beat me into submission."

"You okay, my nigga?" Gar asked him.

"Yeah, I'm straight. Good looking out, I owe you one." He replied, still focused on his victim.

"Ain't about shit, I don't like seeing niggas gang up on mothafuckaz, you feel me? Shoot a nigga the fair one, if anything."

"True dat," He turned around and dapped him up.

"Wash up so we can bounce before them people come."

Lil Man cleaned himself up and left with Gar. From that day forth they were inseparable. You wouldn't see one without the other. They grew to be as tight as him and Lafayette. And when the young nigga finally made it home, Gar put him down with their little crew.

PRESENT

"Y'all heard that nigga Zay came home last week, right?" Lil Man stated.

"For Real?"Gar asked.

"That nigga finna upset the whole hood." Lafayette shook his head. "I know he's making niggaz lay it down. All he and old girl do is steal and rob niggaz. If it ain't nailed down then they're taking it. We ain't gotta worry about'em though, we're small time niggaz. They go after the big fish, not the gold fish."

"I'm not worried either way," Gar assured him. "I'll leave him and that bucket head ho face down in a field somewhere if they try some shit. I'll kill for all of mine, even the scraps. Ain't nobody taking nothing from me, I'll die for my mothafucking shoelaces. It's the principal, my niggaz. Feel me?"

"That's what I'm saying, Gar. We're out here for any fools that want it." Lil Man nodded, poking out his chest. A scraggily looking crackhead wondered over to him. He pulled two rocks from his pocket and swapped it for two crinkled ten dollar bills. The fiend gave him dap and bopped off singing.

"Lalalalalaaa means, I looove youuuuu," he sung, shaking the crack in his fist like a pair of dice.

"Look!" Lafayette nodded down the block to a shiny black object speeding backwards down the street, headed in their direction. When the object got about twenty feet away they realized what it was: a triple black Lamborghini Murcielago. The Lamborghini swung around and started doing donuts in the middle of the street, leaving skid marks in its wake and spewing enough dust to gag Gar, Lil Man and Lafayette. Suddenly, the sports car stopped and sat idle for a time. The purr of its engine was soft and strong. The driver side door lifted up and Cash Out's *'I'm cashin'* out attacked the air. A jeweled hand grasped the doorframe. A Gucci loafer stepped out onto the asphalt, followed by another, and then a 5 foot 9 inch husky frame oozed from out of the vehicle. A mocha skinned man with deep waves, Gucci aviator shades and Gucci vest, started in the homies direction. He beamed brightly and boasted thirty two pearly whites, setting off his goatee. The sun's rays bounced off of the icy Jesus pieces that hung from his neck and created an intense glare that caused Lafayette, Gar and Lil Man to squint. The man approached the trio, his shadow casted on the sidewalk. He greeted the young niggaz with daps and What's ups?

"When did you get her, Shameek?" Lafayette inquired, eyes glued to the $250,000 dollar car. The nigga was smiling like Ace in *Paid In Full* when he saw Mitch in that Saab with the Gold B.B rims.

"Um, about," Shameek glanced at his presidential Rolex, which was flooded with diamonds. "Forty minutes ago, fresh off the showroom floor."

"For real? You turned that Beemer in?" Lil Man asked curiously.

"Nah, I left it at the dealership, I probably have my bitch pick it up in the A.M. It's hers now." he looked to the Lamborghini Murcielago, which was still in the middle of the street, with the engine running and the door up. "What y'all think about that black thang though? All black everything. I call it the funeral service." He whipped out a handkerchief from his pocket and pretended to weep and dry imaginary tears. Everyone laughed except Gar; he had a solemn face, chiseled out of stone. "Lord forgive me, 'cause I'm killing these niggaz out here." He said before busting out into laughter and clapping his hands. When he did this, the icy Jesus pieces hanging from his neck clinked together, like pots and pans. "Y'all like it?"

"That mothafucka tight," Lafayette said, taking in the beautifully crafted machine. He seemed to be in a trance staring at the vehicle.

"That bitch is on hit." Lil Man agreed.

Shameek looked to Gar.

He harped up some phlegm and spat it on the curb. "It's all right." He said, looking unimpressed.

Shameek shot him an expression that said Nigga, you *know my shit is all of that* before draping his arm over Lafayette's shoulders and walking him over to the Lamborghini. "You see this here, youngster? This is what hard work will get chu. You can't get this here nickel and dime hustling, you've gotta elevate your game, nah what I'm saying, my young nigga?" Lafayette nodded his head. Shameek could see that he was hypnotized by the ebony beauty. "She's pretty, ain't she?"

"Nah, she's fucking beautiful," Lafayette admitted, as he circled the vehicle admiring its craftsmanship. "This the baddest broad I done seen in the ghetto, hands down."

Shameek laughed. "Gone and hop in her, Man, take her for a spin."

Lafayette looked up at him as if he were crazy. "Are you serious?"

"Yeah, I'm serious."

"I don't have any L's." he confessed, hating himself for not obtaining his driver's license.

Shameek shrugged. "Shit, I don't have any either, didn't stop me."

Lafayette ran around to the driver side and hopped in, closing the door shut. He strapped the safety belt across his chest.

He gripped the steering-wheel with one hand and held the shifting gear with the other, caressing it with his thumb. Holding down the brake pedal with one foot, he used the other to mash the gas pedal and rev up the engine. The car roared like a great big grizzly bear, bearing its fangs and talons before an attack. The back tires of the $250,000 dollar sports car burned rubber and kicked up dust before shooting down the block, leaving black tire prints on the streets.

URRRRRRRRRRRRRRK!

The hustler came to a halt before the liquor store fifteen minutes later. He threw the Lamborghini in park and lifted the driver side door up. As he stepped out, Shameek approached him with that one of a kind smile, looking like six million dollars. They slapped hands and took another look at the whip together.

"She's a beast, my nigga," Lafayette admitted, "I wish I could whip me something like this."

"And you can, my young nigga. All you've gotta do is get your weight up and stop this nickel and dime bullshit. Youngin' five years ago, I was right where you were, slinging on the corner tryna keep a pot to piss in and a window to throw it out of. It can be done; don't let anybody else tell you different." Shameek looked over both of his shoulders and then told Lafayette , "Come here for a minute." when the hustler approached, he draped his arm over his shoulders and pulled him close, on some big brother shit. "Can you keep a secret?"

"Man, only broads run they mouth."

"Quiet as it's kept, this connect I got sets me out with fifty bricks at twenty a pop, which is a steal since them bitches going for forty racks now a days. I go through them joints in like two weeks and re-up on another fifty. That's a hundred joints every month. I'm letting them birds fly for thirty five a pop to undercut the competition, since everybody else letting them go for the hard forty. I'm the man to come see if you tryna see some real money. Hell, you'd be a fool not to come fuck with me. I'm getting this money."

"You ain't never lied." Lafayette looked from Shameek to his sports car. "Man, this mothafucka is bad, Meek." He rubbed his hand across the back of the Lamborghini.

"La, you're my nigga, I fucks with chu hard-body," he tapped his fist against his left-breast. "So, I'll tell you what, I'ma give you a brick for the low, low. A nigga bless you. Shoot me thirty."

"Thirty, huh?" Lafayette massaged his chin, as he thought on it. Thirty bands for a brick was too sweet of a deal to pass up. He had to take it. The only problem was that he didn't have thirty thousand to put up for the brick. The most he had stashed was ten bands. "Gimmie a couple of weeks to come up with the bag and I'ma get that. There's no way I can let that get past me. Shit, that's the deal of a life time right there, ain't nobody showing that kind of love."

"All right, just come holla at me, La. I'ma put chu down." He slapped hands with the young hustler and patted him on the back.

"All right, good looking out, my nigga," Lafayette watched his hero walk off, stepping off of the curb.

"Y'all niggaz take it easy, Fam." Shameek chucked up the deuce to Gar and Lil Man before hopping back into the Lamborghini. Lil Man threw his head back, but Gar kept a hard-face as he sped off, recklessly.

"What was that nigga talking about?" Gar asked Lafayette.

"Business, big business," He replied, watching the foreign vehicle disappear down the street.

"Well, don't keep an asshole in suspense, spit it out."

Lafayette motioned for Gar to lean in closer. He did.

"Your man said he's gone hit me off with a brick of yay for thirty bands." He told him in a hushed tone.

Gar whistled when he heard the cheap price for the brick, "Straight drop?"

"Straight drop; I only got about ten bands, though. You ain't holding?"

"I got like five bands that I'm sitting on." Gar told him. "But fuck that nigga Shameek, we can just kick in his door and make'em lay it down. I know that pussy sitting on something nice. He probably got some change and a few thangs in the spot, nah what I'm saying? We can make bitch-boy come up off of all his shit." He rubbed his hands together mischievously.

"Nigga, we can't rob Meek!"

"Why in the fuck not?" he frowned and angled his head.

"Meek is cool people, why you wanna hit'em?"

"Man, fuck that batty boy! That nigga come through the hood every other day stunting and fronting. The wolves are out here starving and he's dangling a raw steak in front of'em. He slides through here all breezy and shit, thinking it's all good in the hood! He's begging to be got! And I'm itching to take it! These soft, pussy foot ass niggaz 'round here don't deserve to have nothing! Leave it to a young nigga like me; they'd barely have enough to function."

"So what chu a jack-boy now?"

Lil Man looked between both of his homeboys, listening to their conversation. He was a soldier. Therefore, he took orders and followed them to a T, whatever they decided was cool with him. He was gone roll with it.

"Nigga, I wear a couple of hats." Gar spoke seriously. "Extortionist, drug dealer, jack-boy, kidnapper; I'm whoever I gotta be to get that paper."

"We aren't jacking Meek, and that's final." Lafayette put his foot down. He wasn't about to cross the man that had put him on. Shit, not only had he given him his first shot, but he was about to give him another big break. "I'll think of a way to come up with the paper."

Lafayette swore with determination in his eyes, rubbing his hands together greedily.

***

The sun dipped just below the city streets, leaving the sky a grayish blue. All that could be seen and heard besides the light symphony of traffic, were the bright headlights and the roaring engine of a Lamborghini Murcielago as it ripped through the streets as if it were the assailant of a high speed chase. The driver drove the exotic whip as if he was the last man on earth, and the streets were deserted.

VROOOOOOOM!

Its engine growled as it shot through a stop-light just before it turned red, leaving debris and loose trash floating in the air. The tires wailed when it bent the corner and zipped down a residential block, moving so fast that it ruffled the clothing of pedestrians. The whip didn't slow down until it reached its destination; a gated community just outside of Riverside. The driver stuck his jeweled hand out of the tinted window and punched in the pass code before ascending through the double gates. As soon as he crossed the threshold, he made a left and entered the two car garage of his five bedroom house. Once the garage door shut, he executed the engine and pressed the buttons that released his stash spot. Inside there were about twenty-four bands and a .9mm automatic handgun. He tucked the banger on his waistline and dropped the bands into a South Bay Galleria shopping bag. He then pressed the buttons to close the stash spot and hopped out of the car, brushing the ashes from his blunt off of his shirt. He pressed the button on the remote control on his key-chain and pressed the cell phone back to his ear.

"Yeah, I just made it to my mom's spot," Shameek said into the cell, lying. "I've been running the streets all day stunting in my new toy and making moves. A nigga tired than a bitch. Aww, I miss you too, love, don't trip though. I'ma shoot out there in the morning and we're gone kick it." He claimed, entering through the garage door of his home. He climbed the staircase and headed into his bedroom. "What the fuck?" he bellowed as something leaped on his back, scaring the shit out of him. He drew his iron from his waistline and made to fire over his shoulder, when he heard a woman chuckling. Afterwards, he felt tender kisses being planted on his neck and the side of his face. Right then he knew that it was his side chick.

"Baby, are you, all right?" the woman on the other end of the cell phone asked, worried.

"Yeah, that was my sister playing around; scared the shit outta me." Shameek chuckled, kissing the woman hanging on his back.

"Oh, you gave me a little scare there," the woman said. "Tell baby sis I said hello."

"Wifey says hello," he said to his side chick, who was obviously not his younger sister. She was now straddling him on the bed, sucking and licking on his nipples.

"Tell her I said, hey." The woman said between sucking and licking on nipples of Shameek's muscular body. She was a pretty young thing that closely resembled Rita Ora with her stringy blonde hair and cherry red lipstick. The only difference was she was curvaceous and had the ass of an African Goddess.

"Say, Love, I'ma lay it down," Shameek told his lady. "A brotha's beat. All right, boo, I love you too. Peace," He said before hanging up the cellular and sitting it aside. He picked up the remote to his stereo and pressed play. Instantly, Notorious B.I.G feat R. Kelly *'Fucking you tonight'* came ripping through the speakers, serenading the sexual escapade that was about to take place. Shameek clasped his hands behind his head. He looked down at his side chick as she unbuckled his belt and pulled down his Gucci jeans, exposing his rock hard dick. It was thick and had veins covering it. She licked around the head of his grown man and then engulfed it with her warm, wet mouth. Her devouring of his member drew a soft moan from him and brought a smile to his face. His eyes narrowed into slits as he rode the waves of pleasure.

Chapter 5

Shameek straddled Gemma, the Rita Ora look alike, as she lay topless on her stomach upon the beach blanket. He squeezed the bottle of suntan lotion into his palm. He then rubbed his hands together and rubbed down her shoulders and back, ever so gently. The sapphire in the sky was beaming so bright that her smooth French Vanilla skin glistened when coupled with the lotion. Shameek finished with her back and worked his way down to her white bikini bottom, rubbing around her buttocks and thighs. He could feel the heat coming from her Vajayjay when he coasted along her southern region.

"Mmmmmmm, you better stop." She smiled, tilting her oversized designer shades and peeking over them at him.

What Shameek loved about younger broads is that they always seemed ready to go. It was like they lived to fuck, and since majority of them had been fucking since they were a preteen, they had knowledge on how to make a nigga cum a thousand different ways. What was so sweet about Gemma was that she was barely legal, which meant she wasn't set in her ways and he could mold her to his liking. He'd already had

47

her trained and she was loyal without a fault. See, most cats thought that they were doing something once they got a chicks body, but the kingpin knew that you weren't doing shit until you had their mind. The nigga was a seasoned player, so he knew that. Gemma was so far gone over him that he could have her doing anything that he wanted.

Once Shameek had finished applying the lotion, he rubbed the remainder up his arms and chest. He then leaned over to Gemma, gently kissing on her neck and nibbling on her earlobe. The young lady smiled from behind her shades.

"Why are you playing with my spot knowing that we can't do anything with all of these people out here?" she wiggled her ass. This was something she always did when she was horny.

"Says who?" he asked between kisses on her neck.

"Bae, be serious."

"Don't tell me my ride or die scared. You know daddy don't have no love for weak bitches." He shot her an amused expression.

"You keep on playing and I'ma call your bluff." She grinned and licked her chops seductively.

"Show me what it is then." Shameek brushed her her hair from off of her collarbone and softly bit on the flesh between her shoulder and neck.

Gemma bit down on her bottom lip and her toes curled, obviously turned on. "I feel that chu ready, shit talker, so what's up?" she felt his hardness on her plump ass.

"That ain't me, love," he laughed, "That's my cell." He rose up and pulled his cellular from his navy blue Polo swimming trunks. He looked down at the screen and saw "Baby Love" scrolled across it. *Baby Love* was his nickname for his main lady; at least that's what he led her to believe. She was a very wealthy woman. She worshipped the ground that he walked on and there wasn't anything that she wouldn't do for him. Though Shameek's main lady was ten years his senior, she had a weakness for him. She was under his spell and moved at the beat of his drum. He had her feeling as if she needed him. It was as if she was an addict and he was the drug that she desired. And when she couldn't get her hands on him she felt sick. She'd literally cry and vomit. It was like that song Usher sung back in the day *'You got it bad.'*

"Who is that?" Gemma asked.

"You know who," Shameek pressed 'Ignore' and shoved the cell back into his pocket.

"You're not gonna answer?" Gemma asked, seeing her nigga lying beside her and slipping on his designer shades.

"Nah, I'll get up with her later. I gotta figure out what I'ma tell her since I didn't show up this morning. It's gonna have to be something good. Today was her birthday."

Gemma gasped, tilting her shades down and looking at him like he'd lost his mothafucking mind. "Baby, no you didn't. You could have at least kicked it with her for her birthday." She sympathized with his main chick, because there was no way in hell she would put up with her man missing celebrating her birthday with her. "If you keep on doing this she's going to suspect something."

"You think I don't know that? This is your fault."

"My fault? How do you figure?" she angled her head and raised an eyebrow.

Shameek smiled as he rubbed and pinched her thigh. "You got that wet, wet, Big Daddy can't stay away from it." Gemma's face gave way to a smile hearing that, she loved being told that she had some bomb ass pussy. Shameek leaned forth. Their tongues did a sensual dance before they kissed, locking lips like a couple of teenagers. Pulling away, he smacked her on her right ass cheek and lay back on the blanket, flipping through a DUB magazine.

A volleyball bounced off of Shameek's head and rolled back across the sand. He looked in the direction that it came from and saw a copper skinned woman running towards him, her feet smacking against the warm sand. She had a small waist and long sexy legs. She had on shades and gold Bamboo earrings. Her Coca Cola bottle shape filled out a red bikini. Her big juicy breasts bounced up and down as she ran towards him, buttocks jiggling as she ran along. When she got close enough he noticed her face. It was hell, but her body was heaven.

"Sorry, about that," copper skinned apologized.

"That's all right, love." Shameek grinned. He watched as copper skin ran back across the beach to a muscular built man in sagging camouflage cargo shorts. Copper skin's butt cheeks jumped up one at a time as she ran across the sand, grains of it sticking to the bottoms of her feet. Shameek watched in delight, biting down on his bottom lip and shaking his head. "Lord, have mercy. In Jesus name we pray." He crossed his heart in the sign of the crucifix. Just as a short film was playing in his head of him hitting copper skin doggy style, a smack upside the head brought him back to reality.

He looked over his shoulder and found a frowning Gemma. "What?" he asked with a raised eyebrow.

"You best sleep with one eye open tonight." She warned, mad dogging him.

MEANWHILE

"Was that him?" Zay asked copper skin once she'd returned with the volleyball.

"Yeah, it's him." La'Chat coincided, walking in his direction. "You think we should hit'em tonight?"

"Nah." he told her as they walked beside one another on the beach. "We'll follow him and find out where he lives. There could be patrol cars that come through every couple of hours. He may have an alarm system. Hell, there may even be more than him and her that lives in the place. If this nigga is getting money then he's certainly taking precautions. We have to be on our toes if we're gonna make this move. We'll get'em though." He glanced over his shoulder at Shameek who appeared to be trying to explain himself to a pissed off Gemma. "Oh yeah, we'll get'em."

***

Theo was perched on his cheap sofa putting fire to the end of a glass stem. He sucked on the end of the stem, allowing the white smoke to circulate in his lungs before blowing it back out. He closed his eyes for a moment and then peeled them back open. He looked down into the glass coffee-table at his reflection; his face was covered with small cuts and swollen at his brow and cheek. He showed his teeth and saw that some was either missing or broken. Seeing this, his face twisted in anger and he balled his fists tight. His eyes darted to the beat-up snub nose .38 special with tape around the handle, and for the hundredth time, he thought about hitting the streets to hunt for Batice's baby daddy. As bad as he wanted to catch Gar slipping and clap his ass up, he didn't have a "Killer Bone" in his body. He couldn't see himself killing something or letting anything die. He wasn't about that life. It just wasn't in him. So he decided to deal with his grievances the best way he knew how…by smoking them away.

Theo brought the flame of his Bic lighter back to the end of the stem, cooking the tan rocks packed inside of it and heating up the glass. He absorbed the smoke through his mouth and blew it out of his nose like a riled up bull. The stem got too hot for his finger tips and he fumbled with it until it fell at his feet.

"Damn" Theo cursed. He reached between his legs to retrieve the stem and heard a rap at the front-door. Panicked, he snatched the snub nose from off of the glass coffee-table and shot to his feet. His heart pounded as he crept over to the window. He cautiously peered out from behind the curtains and saw Batice on his porch with her son on her hip. Right then, he unchained and unlocked the door before snatching it open. He stepped aside to allow Batice inside. Once she was in, he stuck his head out of the door and gave the block a quick scan. Satisfied, he closed the door, chaining and locking it back.

"What're you doing here, Batice?" Theo frowned.

"I came to check on you. Are you OK?"

"Does it look like I'm fucking OK?" he pointed to his injured face. "Your baby daddy did a real number on me, but that's all right. I just called up my cousin Loon and we're about to take it to'em." He lied. Ever since he'd met Batice he'd been putting up a front as if he was Gangster 1#. Gar handing his ass to him had crippled his ego, and he felt the only way he could save face was to lay him down. Only thing stopping him from doing so was the finesse and the balls to get the job done.

"Theo, I know you're not talking about killing my son's father." Batice sat Little Gar on the sofa beside her, sucking on his bottle.

"Look at my face," he stepped closer so she could take stock of the damage that was done. "You think I can walk the streets if I let this shit slide? Hell naw!"

Batice was about to respond when a pungent odor overwhelmed her sense of smell. "My fucking head hurts. It smells like burning plastic in here. Are you smoking that shit?" her face balled up.

"Yeah, it was the only way I could calm my nerves." He sat down beside her, resting the hand he held the pistol in on the arm of the sofa.

"Bullshit! As much as you smoke, you're a full fledge head by now." She called him out. "You got some more? Let me take a hit." This drew a strange look from Theo. Lines etched across his forehead and he looked her up and down, like he didn't know who the fuck she was. He'd tried to get her to smoke with him before, but she'd turn him down, opting to blow some weed instead. This was why he found it odd that she wanted to beam up all of a sudden. Now, what he didn't know was Batice was curious about crack. She wondered how the drug could turn people out. Little momma blew a lot of weed and she knew she could quit cold turkey, so she didn't have a clue as to why a crack addict couldn't do the same. She reasoned that they had to be weak minded.

"Are you serious?" Theo asked, scooting closer to her.

"Yes, I'm serious, nigga. Now, are you gonna share or what?"

"Go 'head." He passed her the stem and burned the end of it with the Bic lighter, allowing the flame to lick at the bottom of it. Batice took a big hit like she was a certified crackhead and held the smoke caged inside of her lungs. Her eyes fluttered and she expelled the white smoke from her lips. The feeling she got from the high was almost instant. She felt an eerie sensation, and loved it. Wanting to prolong the experience, she snatched the lighter from Theo and held the flame at the end of the stem. She sucked on the glass penis and drew smoke into her lungs. The second hit was far greater than the one before.

"On the real, Theo, you can't kill Clarence." Batice told Theo, eyes hooded. "We may have our ups and downs, but he's still my baby daddy."

"Uh huh," Theo said, gripping his hardness through his jeans and caressing her thigh. He licked his chops and felt up her baby T-shirt. She smacked his hand away and straightened out her shirt, leaving the back of his hand stinging red.

"I'm serious, Theo, you aren't gonna get so much as a whiff of this pussy if you're contemplating on doing anything to Clarence." She told him, knowing he couldn't get enough of her sex.

Theo sucked his teeth and rolled his eyes. "Girl, please, I ain't stunting that nigga Gar. Ain't nobody gone do nothing to him."

"Swear to God." She told him, sitting up and raising her eyebrow."

"Scouts honor." He held up a hand and crossed himself in the sign of the crucifix.

"Theo, you better not be lying to me."

"I'm not, I put that on everything." He leaned forth, tongue kissing her and unbuttoning her tight fitting white jean shorts. As he dipped his hands inside of her pink, silk panties he could feel the warmth coming from her womanhood. He parted her feminine lips with two fingers and slipped his middle one into her wetness. He closed his eyes for a moment, lapping and nibbling on her nipples as he fingered her. When he opened his eyes he saw Little Gar staring dead at him, prompting him to stop and pull back.

Batice peeled her eyes open and frowned. "What's up?" she asked irritatedly, wanting him to finish what he'd started. Theo nodded to Little Gar. "Oh, he's too little to know what's going on." She picked up the remote control and flipped through the channels until she found Cartoon Network. She then picked up Little Gar and sat him in front of the television; the animated characters had his undivided attention.

"When those cartoons are on, nothing else in the world matters to him." Batice sat

back down beside Theo. He lay back on the sofa and stuffed more crack into the glass stem. He roasted the end of the glass dick with the lighter, as she unbuckled his belt and unzipped his jeans. Her small hand dipped down into his trousers, past his nappy pubic hair and took hold of her prize;

a throbbing seven inch penis with a swollen mushroom tip. It oozed with his mayonnaise. Batice licked her thin lips before wrapping her mouth around Theo's grown man. The next couple of hours they fucked and smoked crack as if they would never get a chance to again after that day.

Chapter 6

Lafayette sat on the roof of his primer painted Buick Regal, drinking a bottle of Minute Maid apple juice and watching the block as Lil Man served crack heads. Gar was leant up against the side of the ghetto classic with his hands stuffed in the pockets of his brown Dickie shorts.

"Yo," he called out to Lafayette, and he threw his head back. "You come up with something yet?" he inquired.

"Nah, I've been thinking on it though. Once we finish up the rest of this work we'll have twenty bands. That means we only have to come up with ten more racks."

"You know I've been chopping it up with Lil Man and…" Gar was cut short by the dirty look Lafayette shot him. He didn't like the fact that Gar had told Lil Man about the dough they were trying to hustle up for the brick. "Don't look at me like that, La. Lil homie is a part of the team; he should know what we're tryna accomplish. I feel like he's earned that much, especially with all the work he's done laid down for the good of the crew."

"Go ahead, man." He told him before taking a sip of his apple juice.

"A smoker gave Lil Man the line on an old Mexican broad down in East L.A; a madam by the name of Isabella Monroe. She manages a brothel that bringing in a considerable amount of cheese. Says she locks away all of the money she takes in for the night inside of a 4-inch-thick, steel safe."

"How much are we talking?"

Gar shrugged. "It varies, man. The smoker broad used to work for the madam until she got strung out. She says she pulls in between one hundred and fifty to two hundred grand, and that's on a bad night. Either way it's a win, win situation. It's way more than we need."

"All right, we can move on it tonight."

"Cool. The sooner the better, I'll let Lil Man know what's up."

THAT NIGHT

Isabella came down the steps one high heel stiletto at a time taking casual pulls from her Virginia Slim. She was a fairly attractive woman in her mid 40s. She had long silky, jet black hair that looked like it belonged in the scalp of a Barbie doll, hazel green eyes and smooth olive skin, free of blemishes. A black mole resided above her lips playing up her sex appeal. She sported a diamond nose piercing and her fingers were decorated in unique diamond rings. Her slim physique was hugged by a black Christian Dior dress that advertised her full succulent breasts and ample ass like a Marlboro billboard surrounded by fluorescent lights at night.

When Isabella reached the bottom steps she could hear Kanye West's *'Gold Digger'* softly playing. She looked around and a smile stretched across her face. She had a full house. Beautiful women walked about; some were dressed to seduce, others were half naked, while the rest were in the nude as they headed to and from the bedrooms. Their customers wore jovial expressions and ruffled clothes. Their necks were littered with hickies and their faces were covered with lip stick imprint kisses. A full house and happy customers meant a lot of money was being made. Isabella's girls drew in doctors, lawyers, athletes and entertainers. The men spent big and tipped even bigger. It was just as Isabella had always said 'There's no business like ho business.'

A knock at the door stole Isabella's attention. She approached it and said, "If sex is a weapon..." she waited for whoever it was on the opposite side of the door to finish the catch phrase, which was the password to enter the brothel.

"Shoot me to death." A manly voice answered.

Isabella unchained and unlocked the door before snatching it open; before her stood a short gentleman in a suit and leather dress shoes. Now, she didn't recognize the short man, but she was happy to see anyone who came to spend money with her.

"I see we have some new money on the floor tonight." She said, extending her manicured hand. "Hello, I'm Isabella Monroe."

"I'm Jackson Turner." The short man smiled and bowed, kissing her hand.

"Pleasure to meet chu."

"Oh, the pleasure is all mine, Ms. Monroe."

"So how did you hear about us?" Isabella inquired.

"A friend of a friend; word travels." Jackson smiled.

"So, I take it you two are familiar with how we go about the payments?"

"Sure am. American Express is OK?"

"More than welcome, right this way." Isabella led them down the hallway and into her office. She closed the door behind him and walked over to her desk. "Why don't you have a seat, Mr. Turner," She motioned to the chairs before her desk.

"Please, call me Jackson and I'd prefer to stand."

"That's fine. Well, what kind of women do you like: black, white, Latina, Brazilian? I have them all." She pulled out another Virginia Slim and fired it up, blowing smoke into the air.

"M.O.B."

"What's that, handsome?"

"Money Over Bitches!" the little nigga drew a .380 on Isabella. "Put cho mothafucking hands where my eyes can see." His eyes took on a menacing appearance and lines formed across the beginning of his nose.

"Who the fuck are you, Busta Rhymes?" Isabella quipped with an attitude, her cigarette dangling at the corner of her mouth as she held her hands in the air.

"No, bitch, I'm a lil nigga with a big black gun! Now, crack open that safe behind that mothafucking Picasso and empty them green backs outta there, before I lay your old pimping ass out in here!"

Isabella laughed and then said, "Let me tell you something, baby, tonight is really not your night. In a few minutes this place is gonna be crawling with cops that're..." she was cut short by a bullet skinning her cheek bone and slamming into the wall, creating a gaping black hole. A sliver of blood trickled down her cheek from the slug grazing her. Her eyes darted back around to Lil Man and his handgun with the silencer attachment on its barrel. It was the look in his eyes that told her that he wasn't for the bullshit and she should oblige his request. "I see you aren't the one for games."

"I'm too old for the games, crack that safe open before I give you a halo out this bitch!" He shot daggers in her direction.

"All right, you're the boss." Isabella told him, right before he snatched the smoldering cigarette from between her lips and mashed it out into the ashtray.

"I know I am." Lil Man placed his gun to the back of her head. "Now hurry up."

***

"You think we should have bust that move with Lil Man?" Lafayette asked. "Shit may get drastic. He may need us."

"Nah, the homie is all right." Gar assured him. "I've got complete faith in him."

"All right, we'll give it a couple more minutes and then we're in there." He said, pulling his banger from underneath his seat and laying it on his lap.

"That's what it is then." Gar agreed, gripping dual .45 automatic handguns. He looked out of the driver side window of the family van at the two-story house. Come on, Lil Man, he thought to himself as he impatiently tapped his All-Star Chuck Taylor Converse on the floor of the van.

You got this, my nigga. You got this.

***

Isabella removed the Picasso painting from the wall and exposed a digital safe. She was just about to press in the combination, but Lil Man stalled her hand.

"Hold up. You may have a burner or something in there to pull out on me. Uh huh, you didn't think a nigga would be up on it, did you?" Lil Man tapped his temple with his finger as he held the gun on Isabella. "Step aside." Isabella moved from in front of the safe. "You make a move and I'll blow your face off. What's the combination?"

"25-37-48." Isabella told him the combination.

As soon as the safe's door popped open, something exploded. Lil Man whipped his face away from the blast, but he was just a second too late. Shrapnel glowing like embers stabbed into the left-side of his face, puncturing his eye and burning cheek. He hollered out in excruciation and staggered backwards, pulling the shrapnel from out of his eye. He then heard Isabella snatch open her desk drawer. Instantly, an alarm blared inside of his head "Gun! Gun! Gun!" with that threat looming in the air, he started clapping off shots blindly and feeling for the door knob.

Just as Isabella reached inside of the desk drawer, a bullet slammed into her shoulder. She hollered out and staggered backwards, removing a chrome .38 with a pearl handle from the drawer. She raised the hand she clutched the pistol in and started getting off. Bullets slammed into the door just as Lil Man was pulling it open, causing small splinters to fly. Through his good eye he could see the house was in total chaos. Naked women and half naked men were running every which way trying to get the fuck up from out of there. Wincing, Lil Man swung back around and let a couple of shots fly inside of Isabella's office to keep her at bay. That shit worked. That bitch dove behind her desk and reached into the drawer she'd taken the small revolver from, retrieving a box of bullets. She dumped the box of ammo out onto the floor and began loading rounds inside of her weapon.

"Garza, where the fuck are you, pendejo? I nearly got my head blown off." Isabella barked into the Bluetooth in her ear, spittle flying from her lips.

Lil Man saw that the doorway was crowded with people trying to get outside. He raised his cannon above his head and cracked two rounds off into the ceiling, causing debris to fall. The roar of his gun made the tricks and whores scatter, leaving a clear path to the doorway. The little nigga ran through the door and leapt from the porch to the bottom of the steps. He landed on his bending knees and ran out into the street, breathing heavily. His vision was blurry and he felt light headed. He wanted to collapse, but seeing the family van heading in his direction egged him on. He knew that this vehicle would be his salvation.

The naked whores and the tricks came pouring out of the house, screaming and hollering. Isabella came out behind them letting her chrome thang rang off at Lil Man. The family van had just come to a halt outside of the house. A bullet whizzed by Lil Man's head and another one shattered the front passenger window, raining broken glass down into the street. Gar hopped out from behind the wheel with his dual .45s pointed in Isabella's direction. The black bangers danced in his hands as they took turns spitting fire at their target. The madam took cover behind a pillar on the porch, letting it take the bullets meant for her. This gave Lil Man enough time to open the vehicle's door and climb inside. Once Gar's .45s clicked empty, Isabella peeked out from behind the pillar to take a shot at him. Seeing this, Lafayette lifted his banger and fingered its trigger. The gun jumped in his palm as he let it cut loose.

"We're out, nigga!" Gar said from behind the wheel of the family van. He'd already loaded his twin .45s and stuffed them into the pockets of his hoodie.

Lafayette hopped back into the front passenger seat. Gar was speeding off before he could pull his foot all of the way inside and close the door. Isabella ran out onto her lawn and fired round after round at the back of the van until her chrome pistol clicked empty.

"Fuck." she cursed and kicked the lawn, sending grass flying.

***

"What the fuck happen back there?" Lafayette asked Lil Man.

"The bitch tricked me, Man! I opened the safe and a bomb or something exploded in my face." He grimaced.

"So was there any money?" Gar asked, looking between the windshield and his homeboy.

"I don't know, Nigga, I didn't get a chance to see."Lil Man gritted as Lafayette held his face and examined his wounds. He gritted harder and clenched his fist so tight that the veins in them bulged.

"We've gotta get'em to the hospital." Lafayette told Gar, focused on Lil Man's face. He was worried about the little nigga'z wellbeing seeing the blood running down his cheek from his ruined eye.

"What the fuck?" Gar said, slamming on the brakes. The family van screeched to a halt. Lafayette looked through the windshield and saw six Mexicans standing outside of a raggedy blue van with choppas pointed in their direction.

Another van skidded to a halt behind them and six more Mexicans hopped out, pointing their assault rifles at them.

"Shit," Lafayette bellowed, seeing the danger that they were in. His heart beat hard in his chest, feeling like it was about to explode.

"Fuck this! Lil Man, you can still shoot?" Gar looked to the backseat. Lil Man nodded and tightened his grip on his .380.

"All right then." Gar went to lift his dual .45s and Lafayette grasped his wrist.

"Don't be fucking stupid, they'll turn this van into Swiss cheese." He gave him a stern look, squaring his jaws and causing them to throb. "Let's just sit tight and see how this plays out." He looked back through the windshield and another Mexican hopped out of the blue van. He was shorter than the rest, but he wore a ski-mask as well. What really made him stand out was his snake skin boots. Reaching back inside of the van, he grasped a feminine hand and helped its owner step on out into the streets. This was Isabella Monroe. The shorter man pointed into the direction of the family van and asked her something in Spanish. She looked to the windshield of the van into Gar and Lafayette's faces, nodding her head. Plaid shirt nodded and switched hands with his choppa approaching the trio. He stepped to the driver side window and knocked Gar out cold with the butt of his assault rifle. Seeing this, Lafayette went take a shot at him, but he was already too late. The little mothafucka swayed his choppa between him and Lil Man daring them to make a move. With that, they took a deep breath in defeat and lifted their hands into the air. The Mexicans had them dead to rights.

AN HOUR AND A HALF

The black pillow cases were yanked from Lafayette and Gar's heads. The light illuminating from the chained bulb above caused them to squint it was so bright. Through narrowed eyes they looked to each other and saw that they were both wearing duct-tape over their mouths. They observed their surroundings and saw that they were down inside of a basement, surrounded by six of the choppa toting Mexicans.

The Mexicans parted and a fifty-five-year-old man in a plaid shirt stepped forth wearing goggles, a black leather smock and yellow dishwashing gloves. He held a chainsaw to his person and yanked the drawstring back. The chainsaw bucked twice before it came to life buzzing loudly. Plaid shirt smiled satanically as he brought the chainsaw forth, his slicked back silver hair shining under the illumination of the chained light bulb. He toyed with Lafayette and Gar, bringing the roaring blade of the chainsaw dangerously close to their faces and then pulling back, laughing maniacally. Lafayette and Gar mad dogged plaid shirt, they didn't so much as flinch when they were faced with death. Plaid shirt nodded his head. He respected the young men's gangster. He killed the chainsaw and set it aside. He pulled off the dishwashing gloves and pulled out a premium cigar. He struck a matchstick across the stubble cheek of one of his henchman and a flame was born, smoke wafting from it. He fired up the over grown cancer stick and fanned out the matchstick, turning it black. He tossed the burnt out matchstick aside and puffed on the cigar, expelling white smoke clouds. Afterwards, he pulled up a chair and sat on it backwards, clearing his throat with his fist to his mouth "You remember me, Lafayette?" Plaid shit asked, smoke from his cigar rising in his face. Lafayette nodded yes, but still kept on mad dogging him. Before he knew it, the duct-tape was being ripped from Lafayette and Gar's mouths.

"Garza Sanchez." The hustler uttered the man's government, tilting his head and glaring up at him.

"That's right." Garza told him, patting his cheek and smiling with the cigar pinched between his teeth.

"Where the fuck is Lil Man?" Gar spat. He was glaring at homeboy too.

"Shut the fuck up, Clarence! Can't you see us talking?" Garza shot him a dangerous look.

"Fuck you, you wetback motha…" Gar was cut short when the drug lord lunged forth and squeezed his bottom jaw so hard that his lips puckered up. There was madness in the older man's eyes and he was sneering, as he brought the ember tip of the cigar towards Gar's right eye. The nigga whipped his head back and forth, trying to avoid the smoldering end of the cigar. "You keep on running your mouth, puto, and I'm gonna burn those pretty brown eyes outta your skull, huh?" Suddenly, he smacked Gar hard as shit across the face, leaving a red palm imprint on his cheek. After that, he settled back down in his chair. He turned back around to Lafayette and said, "Long time, no see. I only wish that it was under better circumstances." He looked over his shoulder to his henchmen. "Me and these negritos go back, they used to smuggle cocaine across the border for me. I knew them both when they were too young to piss straight." He turned back around to Lafayette. "We have a problem. That whore house you guys tried to rob was ran by my sister, Isabella. Your friend ended up shooting her, but don't worry she'll live. Now, she wanted me to take that chainsaw behind me," he pointed a thumb over his shoulder, "and cut off your heads with it. I was gonna do just like she'd told me until I realized I knew you two. That's the only reason why you're still breathing, 'cause otherwise…" He pretended to slice his own throat with his hand. "Out of love and respect for her big brother, my darling sister is willing to let this little mishap pass…f-or a substantial amount of course." He sucked on the end of his cigar and blew smoke rings up towards the ceiling.

"How much?" Lafayette glared at the drug lord.

Garza blew a cloud of white smoke into his face and said, "One hundred thousand dollars."

"A hundred bands? Nigga, are you outta your mind!" Gar spat angrily.

The drug lord looked over his shoulder and said to one of his henchmen, "Miguel, the next time this cock sucker speaks, I want you to shoot him right in fucking his mouth."

"Simon." A Mexican with his hair braided in a long pony-tail replied. His evil eyes peered out of his ski-mask, which had a hole cut out of the back of it for his hair to hang out of it.

"I don't have that kind of dough," Lafayette admitted, "I'ma small time hustler struggling to keep my head above water."

Garza rose to his feet and picked the chainsaw back up. He yanked the drawstring back and the sound of its buzzing saw ripped through the air. He then brought the blade towards Gar's face and he whipped his head around, trying to avoid it.

His eyes were stretched wide open and he was clenchinhg his jaws, veins swollen in his neck.

A nervous Lafayette whipped from a terrified Gar as he tried to avoid the chainsaw to Garza, seeing him bring the blade towards his homeboy's skull.

"OK! OK!" Lafayette shouted, sending spittle flying. He didn't want shit to happen to his man so he'd agree to whatever the drug lord wanted. Garza killed the chainsaw and sat it on his lap once he sat back down in his chair. "I'll get you the 100K. OK? Alright?"

A sweaty forehead Gar shut his eyes briefly and swallowed the lump of nervous in his throat. He took a deep breath and his shoulders slumped, breathing hard.

Garza took the cigar from his mouth and spat on the ground. "I'm gonna give you exactly two weeks to come up with that fedia, Lafayette," he held up two fingers, "Two weeks. If you don't have the dinero by then, I'll gonna send a cleanup crew through that block of yours with orders to lay everything breathing down. Do we understand each other?" the hustler nodded. "Good, 'cause I really like you, you're a good boy. Don't worry about your friend, the little guy. I had my men take him to the hospital. He'll be one eye shorter, but he'll be OK." He rose to his feet and turned to his men. "Untie them and take them where ever they want." He said before headed up the staircase out of the basement.

Gar and Lafayette looked at one another and realized that they were grateful to be alive.

Chapter 7

Lafayette sat at the coffee-table counting money. A smoldering cigarette was wedged between his fingers as he shuffled through the bills. Occasionally, he'd stop to take a pull from his square before he went back to counting the trap. Once he'd finished counting out a grand, he'd run it through the money counting machine, then he'd wrap a rubber-band around it and toss it aside among the other piles of money.

While Lafayette was counting the money, Gar and Lil Man were congregated around the kitchen table, cleaning guns and loading magazines into them.

BEEP!

"That's twenty bands," Lafayette said, lying back on the couch and blowing white smoke into the air.

"We know. That's the fifth time that you've ran the money through the counter." Gar informed him as he loaded slugs into the magazine. "Eighty-five more grand is not gonna magically appear in that machine, we're gonna have to go get it. And if I go get it I'm not finna fork it over to a couple of spics, I'm gonna use it to feed my family. Just as soon as we're finished loading up these straps, me and Lil Man gone hit the streets until we find Garza and his clique; we're slump-ing the whole lot of those faggots. He disrespected the squad and his sister took my nigga'z eye? I'd be damned if I let that slide. I know Lil Man ain't letting that shit slide, are you, blood?"

"Homie gotta get it, G, especially his sister." Lil Man smacked the magazine into his banger and aimed it at some-thing across the room. He wore gauze over his damaged eye, which was held in place by medical tape.

"Y'all niggaz need to chill, now ain't the time to go up against this cat." Lafayette told them. "We don't have the bread we need to have to bring it to'em like that. Y'all seen how that fool's rolling…twelve May Mays deep with choppas; we aren't prepared for what's to come after that. We've gotta get our dollars up first and then pimp slap his ho ass."

"This is some fuck shit!" Gar fumed, jumping to his feet. "This nigga'z gotta go and he's gotta go tonight."

"Straight up," Lil Man agreed. He shot to his feet too.

"Nah, you two hot headed mothafuckaz are gonna listen to me." Lafayette grumbled. "You hit Garza and that shits gonna come back on me, and I'm not playing with my life. We're gonna do this shit my way…that's the only way it's gonna get done."

Lafayette and Gar glared at each other. They were clenching their teeth so tightly that you could see the skeletal bone
structures of their jaws and the veins in their foreheads and
necks. It seemed like an eternity had passed before Gar blew
hard and sat back down at the table, placing his banger upon
it. The hustler had always been the thinker between them and
he was usually right.

Lafayette looked to Lil Man and he reluctantly sat down at
the table.

"All right, oh fearless leader, what bright ideas do you
have to get this paper up for this brick? Inquiring minds wanna
know." Gar folded his arms across his chest.

Lafayette paced the floor massaging his chin, thinking
hard. He looked up and stopped in his tracks. Something
inside of the closet caught his eye. He rushed over to the closet
and grabbed one of the video-tapes from his collection. He ran
back into the living room and sat the tape at the center of the
table. Gar and Lil Man looked from the tape to their homeboy.

"That's how we'll get the money for the block." Lafayette
pointed to the video-tape.

"Man, selling your fuck flicks ain't gone net us no paper."
Gar picked up one of the video-tapes and examined it, tossing
it aside.

Lafayette shook his head and said, "You're a simple ass nigga, you know that? What do all of the bitches have in common that I fuck with?"

"They all have had your dick in their mouths?" he asked, garnering a raise eyebrow from his right-hand man. "What the fuck nigga? I don't know."

"All of their husbands and boyfriends are caked up." Lafayette corrected him.

"So?" Gar shrugged.

"Lafayette, you've lost me," Lil Man said. "What're you getting at?"

"Their significant others are their bread and butter." He told his homies. "Without them they wouldn't have a pot to piss in or a window to throw it out of. They're gonna do whatever they gotta do to keep everything smooth sailing. They know they can't afford to lose them. I'm willing to bet they're willing to pay top dollar so these tapes won't get into their lovers hands." Gar and Lil Man glanced at each other and smiled. "Are y'all with me? We're here now?" he motioned two fingers between his eyes and theirs.

Gar stood to his feet and walked around the table. He grasped Lafayette by the face and said, "La, that's one beautiful fucking mind you've got up there." He kissed his best-friend on the forehead.

"That is a good idea." Lil Man cosigned, nodding.

"What chu waiting on? Call them hoes up." Gar told Lafayette.

Lafayette didn't waste any time picking up his cell and scrolling through his contacts to call up his roster of females.

The women Lafayette called fell through the door two hours later. There were eight of them in all and their ages ranged from twenty-five to forty-three. They were beautiful with bodies that made a nigga want to sing a Keith Sweat song. Their husbands and boyfriends were either big time drug dealers or some big shots in the white collar world. More than a couple of them had asked Lafayette what he'd asked them there for and he told them that he'd explain everything shortly.The hustler had finger foods and cold beverages for the occasion. Once the women had helped themselves to a cup of something and a snack and were seated in a folding chair, Lafayette took the floor and addressed his audience. The living room fell silent and all eyes were on him.

"Now, I am sure you all have been wondering why I've called you here," Lafayette said, pacing the floor with his hands held behind his back, like an old sensai in deep thought. Lil Man was standing to his left eating a peach and Gar was standing to his right with his arms folded across his chest. Lil Man and Gar's eyes watched the room attentively, if any of the women got belligerent than they were prepared to deal with them. "Well, take a good look at the woman sitting beside you and the one sitting beside her, and so on, and so forth. You all have something in common. Do you wanna know what that something is? Sure you do. You've all been getting this dick," he grabbed the bulge in his Jeans and shook it at the women. "It's thick, long and it's good to you. It's real good to you. Well, I've been thinking bitches…"

Hearing the word "Bitches," a tall, slim chick, wearing a Cleopatra wig shot to her feet. Her face was screwed up when she barked, "Hold up, Lafayette, I don't know about the rest of these hoes, but I'm not finna sit up here and let chu call me a bitch!"

"Baby girl, don't be stupid now." Lil Man took another bite out of his peach and held open his jacket, exposing the banger tucked on his hip. Cleopatra wig sat back down in her seat once she saw the big black gun. "Thank you. Go ahead, La."

"Like I was saying," the hustler continued, "I've been thinking, I've been giving all of this good dick away for next to nothing. And I feel it's time that I'm compensated. I want twenty bands a piece from each of you; it's none negotiable. If you're not tryna drop those twenty racks, a video-tape, much like this one will be sent to your lover." He picked up the remote control and turned on the flat-screen. Lafayette appeared on the screen Monkey Fucking one of the women that was in the audience. The women's eyes bugged and their jaws dropped open. They all turned their eyes on the woman who was being sexed on the screen.

"Fuck y'all looking at me for?" a bronze skinned woman with a short hair cut, styled like the old Toni Braxton asked. "I'm not the only one in here he has on tape. You hoes act like y'all shit don't stank."

"Oh, Jesus! I'm coming, I'm coming!" bronze skin said on the screen. Lafayette stood to his feet, his baby arm damn near touching his stomach and glistening from her wetness. Bronze skin's eyes turned to their whites and her mouth fell open. She looked as if an evil spirit had taken possession of her as she sprayed the sheets with her warm liquid.

Lafayette turned off the flat-screen and tucked the remote control into his back pocket. "By tomorrow morning I want twenty bands…cash. Don't bring your ass up here in the A.M talking about you could only get ten or fifteen kay, 'cause I'm not tryna hear that bullshit. I'll ship that mothafucking tape off to your nigga so fast…" he trailed off and shook his head. "Just don't fuck with me. You hand over that paper and your guy will never know his lady is a Five Star Freak, all right?"

"Shit, twenty bands ain't shit to my dude; I can go get that now." One woman said.

"One trip to the bank and I'll have that." Another woman spoke.

"Hell, can we pay you today." A third woman asked.

"Yeah, Lafayette, can we pay you today?" the women asked as a collective.

Lafayette looked to Gar and Lil Man, smiling. They smiled back.

It was time to get paid.

***

Four hours later Lafayette sat back on the couch after counting out the money that the women had brought him back. He looked over the three piles of money while taking casual pulls from his Newport cigarette, polluting the air with nicotine smoke.

"All right, we gotta hundred bands for Garza." Lafayette pointed to the hundred thousand dollar pile of money. "Ninety bands to cop three bricks from that nigga Meek." he pointed to a second pile of money. "And twelve bands to split up between the three of us." He pushed a pile of money to Gar, one to Lil Man and left one for himself.

"Nah, La, I can't take this, this is your loot." Gar pushed the money back to him.

"He's right, La, this is all you." Lil Man pushed his pile back too.

"Uh uh, I gotta spread love to the team. That's what bosses do." Lafayette looked Gar and Lil Man in the face to see if there was any animosity. There was none. This was his operation. He was the king of it and he wasn't sharing the throne. That's why he made sure he paid Gar and Lil Man. He didn't want them to start thinking that there was a partnership between the three of them. He was the boss. He sat at the head of the table. And they were going to be eating off of his plate.

"Well, shit I'm not finna beg a nigga to take money from me." Lil Man said.

"What's our next move?" Gar asked Lafayette as he stacked the racks on top of one another.

"There is no our, I got it from here." Lafayette took a pull from his cigarette and blew out a cloud of white smoke.

It was time to get it cracking.

Chapter 8

THE NET DAY

"It's Lafayette!" Lafayette said over his shoulder out of the window of his primer pianted Buick Regal. There was a buzzing sound and then the double gates opened. He rolled right inside and parked a house down from Shameek's crib. He hopped out of his whip sipping Sprite through a straw of a medium Styrofoam cup and clutching a greasy brown paper bag. He strolled up to the front-door and rapped on it. He heard someone shuffling up to the door. He could feel them looking out through the peephole at him. He heard the chain coming undid and the door being unlocked. The front-door was snatched open and he stood face to face with his plug's pearly whites. He was in a gray Gucci skull cap and matching cardigan sweater.

"What's up, baby boy?" the muscle bound nigga slapped hands with Lafayette as he stepped through the door. He closed the door behind him and motioned for him to sit down on the sofa. "I wasn't expecting to see you so soon; you've been out there doing ya thang, huh?"

"What can I say?" Lafayette grinned and sat his cup of Sprite on the table. "I brought you something to eat." He tossed the greasy brown paper bag to him. Shameek twisted his face and held up the brown paper bag.

"Fuck you got in this bag, a Philly cheese steak? You know I don't eat meat, I'ma vegan, nigga."

"Take a look inside." Lafayette sat back on the sofa sipping on his Sprite.

The kingpin shrugged and opened up the brown paper bag. That pearly white smile of his made another appearance as he pulled out two of the thick bands that were inside. "This is more than thirty." He declared.

Lafayette nodded and said, "That's right, I want three of them White Girls! You told me to step my game up, my nigga. Well, here I am." He opened his arms like a field goal was good.

"And that's why I fucks with chu." Shameek tapped his fist to his heart before carrying the brown paper bag off. "I'll be right back."

Lafayette watched as the muscle bound man headed down the hallway as he sipped on his Sprite. He figured he must have been going to put the money up and then going to get the blocks of cocaine. Lafayette raised an eyebrow when he saw the kingpin duck off into the kitchen. He wondered where he kept his stash at if not inside of his bedroom. He didn't have any plans to rob him, he was just curious. Shameek had been giving him game since he'd known him and he wanted to see what else he could pick up. As quietly as he could, he sat his cup down on the table and crept to the kitchen doorway. He peeked inside and saw him enter the pantry. Lafayette snuck over to the pantry doorway and peeked around the corner. Shameek approached the back wall inside of the pantry and pushed aside a box of Honey Nut Cheerios, flipping the silver switch hidden behind it. The back wall slid upward and exposed a shelf of eight blocks of cocaine. He dropped the three blocks of cocaine into a Macy's shopping bag, one by one. Lafayette hurried out of the kitchen and back into the living room, where he sat back down on the sofa. He picked up his cup and withdrew his cellular, pretending to look through it when Shameek emerged from the kitchen. It wasn't until the kingpin sat the shopping bag on the coffee-table that he looked up from the cell phone's screen.

"This me?" Lafayette pointed to the shopping bag.

"Yep, that's you," he answered, sipping on a glass of Cognac he'd poured before leaving the kitchen.

Lafayette set up cup down and put his cell phone up. He then peeked inside of the bag. At the very top there was a block of cocaine wrapped in hot pink Seran Wrap. Its stamp was a cartoonish bee wearing a Tiara and holding a royal scepter with "Queen Bee" emblazoned across it.

"All right, Shameek, I'm outty five thousand." Lafayette rose to his feet.

"Oh, come on, baby boy, kick it and have a drink with me for a minute."

"I've gotta take a rain check, fam. We'll have plenty of time to do us; right now I'm on this paper chase. You know how it is." He slapped hands with him.

"Indeed I do." Shameek responded, indulging in his alcoholic beverage as he watched Lafayette head for the door. A grin emerged on his face thinking of how the younger version of him was going to grind his way up to legendary status in the streets.

THAT NIGHT

"You got it?" Gar asked as he came out of the house.

"Is a pig's pussy pork?" Lafayette smiled as he reached the back of his Buick Regal. He popped the trunk and lifted it. He was about to reach inside to grab the Macy's shopping bag with the blocks of cocaine in it, when Gar stopped him.

"Watch out, La!" He told him. At that moment a bright light shined in Lafayette's face, blinding him. His eyes narrowed into slits and he raised a hand above his brow, trying to see where the fluorescent ray was coming from. There were two blue eyed, hard-face police officers staring dead at him. The officer on the passenger side chewed on his gum as he eye fucked Lafayette. The hustler's heart skipped a beat and he saw his life flash before his eyes. He was about to make a run for it, when the light vanished and the police cruiser slowly pulled off.

"That was a close call." Gar watched the police cruiser roll off and waved the middle finger behind it.

"Phew." Lafayette crossed his heart in the sign of the crucifix, relieved that the police chose to find some other poor soul to fuck with. He snatched the Macy's shopping bag from out of the trunk and slammed it shut. "You find us a cook yet?" he asked Gar.

"Yep, Lil Man's auntie. Well, she's not his real auntie, but she used to run with his mother back in the day."

"Is she any good?"

"He vouches for her, and she sho' 'nough talks a good game. We'll see, though."

"Come on, let's get up in here," Lafayette threw his arm over Gar's shoulders and headed towards the house. "I got this banger on me and three bricks of yay. That's enough to finish a nigga off for life."

When Lafayette came through the door he saw Lil Man sitting at the kitchen table talking to whom he assumed was his auntie. She was an overweight, high yellow woman with very bad skin. She looked to be in her mid sixties but she was only forty-seven; her hard knock life had aged her considerably. She had a diamond stud in her nose and wore a tattered reddish blonde wig, which she wore a beige bandana around. The imprint of her long floppy breasts could be seen in her red Fubu T-shirt.

Lafayette patted Lil Man on the shoulder as he past him.

"What's up, La? This my people, right here." Lil Man motioned towards his auntie. "She wants to get down with the team."

"Hey, I'm Renee, everyone calls me Auntie." She waved a chubby hand.

"What's up, Auntie?" Lafayette sat the Macy's shopping bag at the center of the table and sat down in the chair. He took an apple Blow Pop from his jacket pocket. He removed the wrapper and slipped the lime green orb between his lips. "Now Lil Man says you're tryna get down with us. What I wanna know is what would make you such an asset to our squad?" He took the three bricks from out of the Macy's shopping bag, stacking them on top of each other. Lying back in his chair he saw a look in Auntie's eyes that he was all too familiar with. It was the look of a crackhead deprived of its habit for far too long. Acknowleding this, Lafayette took a mental note of it and deposited it into his memory bank.

"Auntie," Lil Man's nudged her.

"Huh?" she asked, coming out of the hypnosis the white powder had put her under.

"The man asked you a question." Lil Man said.

"Oh, right. 'Cause my whip game is proper." Auntie took a pull from her cigarette and blew out a cloud of white smoke. "I got the hand of God when it comes to whipping coke into crack, baby, real shit. I can whip them three white hoes you got there into six lily white bitches." She said confidently.

"I hear you talking, hot shit, but chu gotta make me a believer." Lafayette said to her. He pulled the sucker out of his mouth and eyed it admiringly as he talked to her. "Lil Man, give her an ounce and let's see what see can do. Gar, snatch up a smoker, anyone will do. We need someone to tell us if old head's recipe is on the money."

"I'm on it." Gar headed out of the door.

"Everything you need is under the kitchen sink." Lafayette told Auntie.

Auntie mashed her cigarette out in an ashtray and dipped into the kitchen.

***

"Somebody's fa' sho' 'nough home," Zay said as he stared at Shameek's well lit home. He and La'Chat were parked a few houses down from it. They'd entered the gated

community behind a Benz station wagon that had arrived at the same time that they had.

"Think it's just him and the girl inside?" La'Chat asked. She took a pull from a smoldering L and passed it to Zay. She blew out a stream of white smoke and pulled green latex gloves over her hands, flexing her fingers.

After taking a few hits of the L, Zay blew white smoke from his nose and mashed it out in the ashtray. "It don't even matter," he began, "I done seen the hardest fold their hand when faced with this big mothafucka." His gloved hand held up his .357 Magnum revolver. He pulled a ski-mask over his head and so did La'Chat. She pulled her Desert Eagle from underneath the seat and cocked it. She grabbed Zay by the back of the neck and pulled him close. They kissed hard and passionately before hopping out of the stolen whip.

Just another day at the office.

MEANWHILE

He brought his ashy chapped lips to the end of the glass stem. His dry, burnt finger tips gripped it firmly as he held a lighter to the bottom of it, allowing the flame to lick at it. The reddish orange flame cooked the tan rocks and caused white smoke to manifest. His chapped lips sucked on the end of the glass dick, vacuuming the white smoke into his mouth and filling his lungs. He sealed his lips tightly and held the smoke a moment before blowing it back out.

"Yo, is that shit official?" Lafayette asked, standing before him, a line creasing his forehead.

The crackhead peeled his lips open and exposed his yellowing, red veined eyes. He scratched his neck and rubbed his nose with the palm of his hand. He nodded and said, "Yeah, this is some pretty decent work you got on your hands here," before lighting up the stem and sucking on the end of it again. The smoke wafted around his face, obscuring the others view of him.

"I told you my peeps ain't no joke in the kitchen." Lil Man said to Gar who was standing beside him.

"All right, I'll give you your props." Gar smirked and dapped him up.

"So what's up? Am I down?" Auntie asked, wiping the sweat from her brow with her latex gloved hand. She then went on to fill a glass with faucet water from out of the kitchen.

"Yeah," Lafayette nodded, "you're down. Let me ask you a question, though, just outta curiosity."

"Shoot." Auntie said, taking a sip from her glass of water.

"Who taught you how to cook?"

"My husband, may he rest in peace." Auntie said. "You may have heard of'em, Bernie Ward ring a bell?" Lafayette shook his head no, so she continued on. "He was a hustler from back in the day. He showed me how to work them pots 'cause he needed help cooking and didn't trust anybody else with his work. He caught a bid and ended up getting killed in prison. I fell into depression, ended up trying the stuff and got hooked on the shit. And here I am today. Now if you don't mind, I'd like to get back to work."

"By all means," Lafayette held up his hands in surrender. "Gar, escort this gentleman outside." He said of the crackhead that was still getting high, smoke still wafting all around him. "Lil Man, let me holla at chu." He walked with Lil Man to the corner of the living room. "I noticed your peoples gotta itch, I want someone in here with her and the product at all times."

Lil Man nodded. "I got chu faded."

"Good. Let's eat." He held out his fist and smiled.

"Let's eat." The little nigga dapped him up.

Chapter 9

In two weeks Lafayette had blown through most of the kilos. He had the block jumping like a tip off. His dimes looked like twenty dollar pieces and his nickels looked like ten dollar pieces. The crackheads were getting more bang for their buck. With every dollar they got they were running to his trap to score. It looked like there was a block party going down every day on 27th street. The traffic was getting so heavy that Lafayette had to open up another trap and put more workers on. The number of crackheads coming through was drawing the polices' attention, so he paid a few of the badges off to look the other way.

"This shit is crazy, La," Gar began, "   Two weeks ago niggaz was nobodies, but now we're climbing the ladder. Today it's these two little blocks, tomorrow it's this whole hood." He smiled as his eyes took in the block and the crackheads coming to and from the trap down the street. Today was a beautiful day. He was young, alive, and on his way to being hood rich.

"That's how the game is, my nigga. Today you could be down bad, tomorrow you could be back up." Lafayette said, sitting on the stoop. "It's our time."

"We got now and forever, I'ma 'bout to put this mothafucka in a yoke, and I ain't never letting go." Gar kneeled down to his man and slapped hands with him. "We're taking over; cats may as well kiss the game goodbye."

Lafayette grinned and nodded in agreement. "What's up with that other chef, though? It's time to see my man."

"Lil Man over there with her right now, if she's as good as Auntie then she's on."

"You trust Lil Man's judgment?" Lafayette inquired.

"Shit, he brought us Auntie, didn't he?" Gar said. "She's a fool with them pots; she needs to bring out her own line of cookware or some shit."

"The Martha Stewart of the ghetto," Lafayette chuckled and dapped up that nigga Gar. He felt his cell vibrate in his pocket and pulled it out. He looked down at the screen as the device danced in his hand. The name on the display was "Garza". Lafayette made a funny face, pressed *Ignore* and slipped the cell phone back into his pocket.

"Who dat?" Gar asked, shadow boxing.

"Garza."

"You thought about how you're gonna handle that shit?"

"Yeah, fuck him. I'm not giving him shit. I was just thinking about how many more bricks we can get with that hundred bands."

"See, me and you are here now." Gar motioned two fingers between him and his homeboy's eyes, "We're here, you seeing what I'm talking about."

"Yeah, man, fuck that nigga! He want a war then we'll give'em one!" Lafayette twisted the toothpick around in the corner of his mouth.

"I got my bangers and I know my Ace got his." Gar turned his eyes on him.

"You know I stay with that." Lafayette lifted his Trukfit shirt and flashed the 17 shot .9mm automatic residing on his hip.

"That's what's up, we're out here." He dapped him up.

Garza fucked with the bull, now he had to get the horns.

LATER THAT NIGHT

"It's a go." Lil Man rubbed his hands together greedily and licked his top lip. "Homegirl gotta whip game just as good as Auntie's."

"All right, cool," Lafayette replied. "She can help knock out these next few blocks I'm finna get."

"Yo," Lil Man tapped him. "Old girl was hoping that she could get an advancement to get a couple of groceries; lil momma got two youngins and shit, fam." Lafayette nodded and peeled off a few dead white men and handed them over to Lil Man. He'd just stuffed the bills into his pocket when a silver GT Bentley pulled up. The tints were so dark that you couldn't see inside.

"Who dat?" Lil Man asked Gar in a hushed tone, brows furrowing.

"Gangsta," he replied without taking his eyes off the Bentley.

The driver side door of the Bentley swung open and a caramel complexioned man in an Armani suit stepped out. The suit hugged his massive arms. His bulky body would have you thinking one of two things: he was a professional body builder or he'd done a stretch in some up state correctional facility. Gangsta was a stern yet fair business man, but when drama flared he'd shed that skin to become a smooth and calculating killer. He adjusted his tie and stepped upon the curb, making his way towards the trio.

"Fuck you think this nigga wont?" Lafayette asked Gar, keeping his eyes on the nigga in the suit that was advancing in their direction.

"I don't know, but we're about to find out." Gar said, standing up to greet Gangsta.

Gangsta was a drug dealer and the shot-caller of the Eastside Outlaws Rolling 20s Bloods Gang. The homies bought their drugs from him and only him. If they didn't then they paid a tax to hustle on his corners. He didn't allow anything to move in his little section of The Low Bottoms without getting a piece of the action. That's how he made it and that's how it was. His reason for paying Lafayette a visit was just that.

"What's up, Blood?" Gangsta slapped hands with Lafayette.

"What up?" the hustler replied.

Gangsta threw his head back at Lil Man and Gar and they returned the gesture. They all knew each other and respected one another.

"To what pleasure do I owe this visit?" Lafayette inquired.

"Business," Gangsta told him. "Everything is always business." Lafayette shrugged. Gangsta looked down the block at the crackheads heading to and coming from the trap house. A grin emerged upon his face. "How long have our families known one another?"

"Shit, forever. My folks moved here in the summer of '57."

"And mines the winter of '53," Gangsta informed him. "My daddy and your grand daddy used to work at the same steel mill together. My mother and your grandmother worked for the same Italians downtown, knitting blankets and quilts. Hell, your brother's looking at doing a bid on my behalf right now. He's been in that cage two years and has yet to open his mouth." Lafayette's identical twin brother, 8-Ball, was busted inside one of Gangsta's trap houses with a quarter of a bird and a pistol. He took his charge on the chin and kept his mouth shut. Gangsta respected him for standing tall in a game full of snitches and shady characters. In return the O.G promised to take care of his family and keep his commissary full.

Lafayette took a deep breath and folded his arms across his chest. "I hear you, O.G, but what're you getting at?"

"I reside over this hood. The twenties are mine. I allow everybody over here to eat, just as long as they pay tribute. Everyone has to throw in their lot, there aren't any passes this way. No matter whom they're related to. I sat back and chilled while y'all were doing y'all thang over there by the lil liquor store 'cause it was Cibbles and Bits; short paper. This block you got here is doing numbers. It's time you kicked something up to the powers that be."

"So what's this? A strong arm?" Lafayette chuckled and looked to his homies.

"This ain't no strong arm, my nigga." Gangsta held up his hands in surrender. "This is how this republic operates under my jurisdiction. I'm surprised you haven't become familiar; Gar is from the hood, he knows how it goes."

"True dat," Gar admitted. "The homie's on the up and up."

"See, this ain't no strong arm, this is the way it goes. Everybody has to kick something in." Gangsta said. "If this was a strong arm I would have had my Y.Gs come through this block like a parade, laying bodies down. Then I would have told you to start kicking me down every week, or I was gone make it so hot around here that you wouldn't be able to get so much as a nickel rock off. But our family has history that's why I stepped to you instead of sending my young wolves. You know these young Eastside niggaz be wild as shit, they don't know how to act."

Lafayette was born and raised in The Low Bottoms. He grew up on 27th and Griffith in a big white house on the corner. Though nearly every one and their baby momma were from Eastside Rolling 20s Bloods, including his older brother, he never got quoted on. He never did dig gangbanging. It didn't make sense to him. The colors war wasn't going to put money in his pocket or add inches to his dick, so he wasn't for throwing in his lot with the rest of the lost souls. His only mission in life was to get rich or die trying. He had it in mind to tell Gangsta to stick his taxes up his ass, but he was getting money now and didn't want to rock the boat. Besides, he didn't have as many guns on his side as the O.G. Lafayette was sure the soldiers he could rally would give the shot-caller hell, but how long would it last before their flames were all blown out? His cooler head prevailed thinking that if being taxed was the way of the land then he'd abide. He was beginning to see some real money coming his way and he wasn't trying to fuck it up before he really got to enjoy it.

"What's the quota?" Lafayette asked.

"Two grand at the end of every week, that's on the love." Gangsta told him.

Lafayette nodded and said, "All right," before slapping hands with the O.G and patting him on the back. He then watched him slip back into his Bentley and drive off. He kept his eyes on the silver vehicle as Gar stepped down beside him. "I just got robbed without a gun; two bands a week."

"You didn't get robbed, La, everybody has to break bread." Gar told him. "Think of it as the price of doing business."

Lafayette turned around to Gar wearing a serious expression. "We've been homies for a long time, and I've never questioned your loyalty. But I have to know…If I decide to go against the grain are you gone hold it down or ride with Blood?"

"I'ma hold it down with my brotha," Gar said with a face as serious as Lafayette's.

"Brothas," Lil Man entered their fold, wearing a serious expression.

Lafayette slapped hands with his mothafucking niggaz.

All for one, and one for all.

MEANWHILE

Batice had just gotten out of the shower and wrapped a towel around her body.

Using her hand, she wiped a circle in the fogged mirror and revealed her reflection. She'd lost a considerable amount of weight and it made her head seem huge. The size of her dome coupled with her body made her resemble a human Bobble Head Doll. Seeing her former self deteriorating was depressing for Batice. She knew that it was because of the crack, but she couldn't bring herself to stop. She thought she could use the drug recreationally like she did with weed, but it proved to be much more addictive. She found herself wanting to smoke every hour on the hour. She needed crack like she needed oxygen, and she felt that she would die without it.

When Gar noticed the change in her appearance she told him that her youngest uncle, Roger, had died. What she had told him was the truth but they didn't have much of a bond for her to feel anything about his passing. Her uncle's death was the perfect excuse for her to be away from home, claiming to be clearing her head while she was really getting high with Theo.

When Gar would get up to go hustle, Batice would drop their son off at her mother's house and dip off to Theo's place. Theo used her body for sex and she used him for the crack he had. It was a fair exchange. He got what he wanted and she got what she wanted. Theo knew what floated Batice's boat and he made sure he always had it on deck. He could get her to do whatever sexual act he could imagine just as long as he had those precious rocks in his possession.

Batice tossed the towel aside she'd used to dry her hair and headed into her bedroom. She picked up the white cordless telephone and punched in a number. She pressed the cordless phone to her ear and waited for someone to answer.

"What's up, Theo? Did you make it home yet?" Batice said into the phone, squeezing a lotion into her palm so she could lather herself down. "Yeah, I got the wet, wet, you got what I need?" she smiled. "Cool, I'm on my way." She hung up.

Chapter 10

THE NEXT NIGHT

Lafayette sat behind the wheel of his Buick Regal munching on a Whopper and fries as he stared out of the windshield. Gar played the front passenger seat sipping strawberry Fanta from a Burger King cup. His eyes were focused through the windshield as well. He and his right-hand were watching the corner. They had a couple of young niggaz out there going hand to hand. Across the street from him in a tan apartment building were two other cats spying on the block through binoculars. Directly across the street from the apartment building was two cats that looked like they were just shooting the shit, but in all actuality they were there to hold the hustle down. Lafayette had this set up on a couple of blocks. His operation was running smoothly, like a well oiled freight train.

"It's looking like The Walking Dead out this bitch." Gar commented on all of the crackheads roaming throughout the neighborhood.

"It's the most beautiful sight in the ghetto." Lafayette smiled proudly. "I keep the heads fed and my crew is eating. Everybody is happy. Shit is lovely."

"True indeed."

"Look at Lil Man, old dog ass nigga." Lafayette looked at his homeboy with disgust.

After emerging from out of the liquor store with a bottle of something concealed inside of a brown paper bag, Lil Man ushered a thick crackhead chick with a strong face into an alley. He looked both ways before ducking off into the dark path. He screwed the top off whatever he had in the bag and took it to the head, guzzling it. His throat rolled up and down his neck as he indulged. Once he'd gotten finished, he un-zipped his jeans and pulled out his meat. He placed his hand on top of the perm headed smoker's head and lowered her to him knees. Yeah, that's right, Lil' Man was gay. Anyway, he took swallows of the alcohol beverage concealed inside of the bag and held the back of the fiend's neck, observing him giving him a sloppy wet, blow job.

"Disgusting mothafucka," a smirking Lafayette shook his head. "He could have at least strapped up, ain't no telling where that smoked out ass nigga done been."

"What? You ain't know?" Gar asked, wearing an amused expression. "That's Lil Man; his dick has boldly gone where every man's dick has gone before. My man don't give a mad ass fuck. He'd stick his wang inside of a python's mouth if you held its mouth open for'em."

"You tell that lil nigga that if he keeps rolling the dice he's bound to crap out one of these days. The Lord protects fools and babies, but how many times are you gonna stick your hand into the fire before your ass realize you can get burned?"

"Aye, you only live once." Gar looked away from the gay ghetto porno playing outside of the passenger side window.

"Which is reason enough to take precautions."

Feeling his cell phone vibrate, Lafayette dipped into his pocket and pulled it out. "Garza" was on the screen; he quickly pressed 'Ignore' and slipped his cellular back into his Dickie pocket. When he looked up he saw a van with its headlights out, approaching cautiously. This made him suspicious.His face balled up and he tapped Gar on his arm, pointing to the windshield at the creeping van. "Who this right here?"

"I don't know, nigga sho' is creeping though." Gar frowned as he tried to peer inside of the van. He placed his banger into his lap and so did Lafayette.

Meanwhile, Lil Man zipped up his jeans and dipped his hand into his pocket. He pulled out a couple of crack rocks and dropped them into the crackhead's dry, ashy palm. He then picked up his bottle of liquor and smacked the fiend on his ass as he walked out of the alley, pulling a Murphy from out of his ass. Lil Man was stepping out of the alley with the bottle turned up when the van coasted through the intersection. His eyes darted in the direction that the van went. He then brought the bottle down from his lips and wiped his mouth with the back of his fist. There was something eerie about the vehicle that had his undivided attention.

"Yo, that's the van that the eses snatched us up in that night." Gar recalled.

"Sho' in the fuck is." Lafayette concurred, still focued on the van.

As soon as the words left his mouth the van picked up speed, causing its tires to screech. Its side door slid open and AK-47s emerged, the rays of the light posts kissing off of them. The sight of the assault rifles put everyone on high alert. Crackheads and D-boys scattered everywhere. Niggaz and bitches were running across one another as they tried to get the fuck from out of the away. The AK-47s spat hot fire, lighting up the night and making the hood sound like a Vietnam War zone. Bullets tore off limbs, hands and exploded the domes of crackheads. Blood was flying everywhere and shrills of agony filled the air. The howls and cries of men and women sounded throughout the darkness. One D-boy covered his head and ran down the block trying to avoid a hot one. The gunners that were posted across the street chased after the van letting slugs fly from their bangers. The rounds exploded the back windows of the van and hollowed its rear, ruining it with what looked like a million holes. One of the shooters on board the van pushed its door further open and released a spray that left the gunners soiling the street, specks of burgundy littering the asphalt.

A bullet whizzed by Lil Man's face and he saw sparks fly by his eyes. He dropped the brown paper bag and the bottle it concealed shattered, turning the wet part of the bag a darker brown. Instantly, he drew his strap. He went to turn around, when his face was plastered with the blood and brain matter of the crackhead that had just sucked him off. His face balled up and he looked like he had eaten something sour. Before the smoker's limp body could hit the surface, he wrapped his arm around his neck and pulled him into his body, using him as a human shield. The little nigga let his thang off while the corpse of the crackhead absorbed the shots that were meant to rob him of his life. Lil Man's handgun wasn't a match for the assault rifles, but he managed to let a lucky shot off. A lonely bullet crashed into one of the shooters faces and he fell out of the van, rolling along the street. His lifeless body looked like a rag doll as it tumbled along the white lines that made up the lanes.

Lil Man allowed the crackhead's body to fall before taking cover beside a Honda station wagon. He took the time to eject the spent magazine from his banger, letting it clasp to the ground. He was about to inject a new one, when a shooter stepped out from behind the Honda. He smiled wickedly as he pointed his AK-47 at Lil Man. The little nigga'z eyes bugged and his stomach dropped. He felt the stench of Death looming over him, but then a miracle happened, the shooter was laid down by a serious case of lead poisoning.

BLOC! BLOC! BLOC! BLOC!

The shooter lay sprawled on the sidewalk as red streams ran from his form and absorbed into the cracks and crevasses of the sidewalk. Lil Man whipped around and Lafayette gave him a nod, letting him know he had his back, gripping his smoldering 17 shot .9mm. Beside him was Gar, letting his twin .45s go at the same time.

When Gar started to draw more fire from the choppas than he could handle, he stooped down beside the blue Corsica he'd taken cover behind. His twin.45s wafted with smoke that evaporated into the cool night's air. Lafayette ran up to the hood of the Corisca and aimed his banger at the tinted driver side window of the van. He closed his left-eye, waited a moment, and then squeezed the trigger. His weapon jumped as a fire ball erupted from its barrel and shattered the black glass of the driver side window. The van lost control and slammed into a telephone post, nearly uprooting it. The van's cargo of shooters abandoned their transportation and scattered through-out the neighborhood. Lafayette, Gar and Lil Man opened fire on the fleeing shooters, but their AK-47s kept them at bay. A shriek in the darkness drew Lafayette, Gar and Lil Man's attention. They turned around and a Mexican man was stand-ing over the D-boy, hacking away at his hand with a machete.

"Raaaahhh! Haaaa! Gaaahh!" the wide eyed D-boy hol-lered aloud, as the shiny blade was swung down at him. Each swipe of the leatha weapon sent a severed finger flying, and lastly, a thumb. Blood speckled the victim's clothing as well as his attacker, whose unmerciful eyes could be seen through the holes inside of his ski-mask. His crooked, gritting teeth shown through the mouth in the mask. He swung the machete back and forth with all of his might until there wasn't anything left besides a bloody stump.

"Grrrrrrrr," The Mexican man gripping the machete lifted it above his head. His eyes danced with murder so his victim knew that his time had come.

"Aaaaahhhhh," The D-boy hollered, tears threatening to drip from his eyes.

"Noooooooooo," Lafayette yelled letting his thang go. Each shot that it released caused it to recoil in his hand.

BLOC! BLOC! BLOC! BLOC!

Bullets deflected off of the building that the Mexican man was standing before, sending chunks of matter and debris flying. The Mexican man sheathed his blade and grabbed the D-boy by the front of his shirt, pulling him towards the van behind him.

"Help me! Somebody heeelllp me," the D-boy screamed bloody murder.

Two more shooters hopped from the van and spraying their assault rifles, making Lafayette, Gar and Lil Man take cover. Police car sirens filled the air as they were approaching hastily. Once the slinger was dragged inside of the van, the door was slid closed and the van sped off.

"Come on!" Lafayette yelled out to Gar and Lil Man as he hopped behind the wheel of his Buick. Once Gar and the little nigga were on board, the hustler fired up the engine and gunned his Regal down the trashy alley; his bright headlights resembling orbs leading the way.

***

Lafayette paced back and forth across his living room floor with his hands behind his back, plotting his next move.

"Damn, did you see how that Mexican fool did Lil Ace?" Lil Man spoke on the young D-boy that the Mexicans had snatched up, shaking his head. "He was hacking away at his fucking limb as if it were a celery stick. Dude is only sixteen; do you think they killed him?"

"Nah, they didn't kill'em yet, they snatched him up for a reason." Gar reasoned, "If they were just gonna murk him he would have gotten his issue right there on the block."

"This is true." Lil Man nodded.

"Fuck man!" Gar slammed his fist into his palm. "We've gotta get active with these niggaz."

"This mothafucka Garza is connected to one of the biggest cartels in Mexico; you know them May Mays don't play." Lafayette let them know. "They be busting on Binem over there like they're regular niggaz and shit. Last year I heard they chopped off a police chief's head and tossed his body dead smack in front of the precinct; straight G with it." He slipped a Newport between his lips and went to fire it up with a Bic, when he felt his cellular vibrate in his pocket. He dipped his hand into his pocket and looked at his cell phone. "Garza" was on the screen. He looked from Gar to Lil Man. "This him."

"Answer it, nigga." Gar asked.

Lafayette shut his eyes, took a deep breath and pressed "answer". He brought the cellular to his ear and said, "What's cracking?" before taking a pull from his cigarette.

"So this is what it takes to get chu to answer your phone, huh? I should have done this sooner." Garza smiled knowing that he had the upper hand in the situation. Lafayette could hear the saliva move in his mouth as his lips formed the amused expression.

"Well, you got my attention, now what?"

"Now you give me my money, it's double now. I want $200,000 dollars for the inconvenience."

"Where am I supposed to pull another hundred grand from? My ass?" Lafayette asked heatedly. He was so angry that he involuntarily gripped his cellular tighter, causing his hand to turn white at the knuckles.

"You can pull it from outta your mother's cunt for all I care, negrito! But you better have it by tomorrow night or else!"

"Or else what?"

"Lafayette?" Lil Ace's weak voice came on the phone.

"Lil Ace is that you, homie?" Creases formed on Lafayette's forehead.

"Yeah, I…"

Snikt!

Thud!

"Gaaaahhhh," Lil Ace's screamed in agony so loud that it caused Lafayette to wince and snatched his ear away from his cell phone. When Garza came back on the phone, Lafayette could still hear his little homeboy hollering out in the background.

"That's what was left of your friend's right-arm!" Garza growled, pissed the fuck off now. His black hearted ass wasn't smiling now. Nah, he'd gone from zero to one hundred real quick. "You keep testing my gangster, and I'll take his left-arm, his right-leg, then his left-leg until nothing is left besides a bloody torso! Do we understand each other, mayate?"

"Yes, we understand each other." Lafayette replied sub-missively. He'd just gotten an understanding of who was the boss. Whether he liked it or not Garza was in control.

"Good. I'll call you tomorrow with the location and time." Before Lafayette could reply, the phone was hung up in his ear.

"Fuck happen? Was that Lil Ace screaming?" A frowning Gar approached his man.

The hustler nodded and said, "They hacked off what was left of his right-arm," then massaged the bridge of his nose, shaking his head sadly. Gar looked away hating to hear what had been done to their little homeboy. Lil Man shook his head hearing what had been done. "He said if I don't give'em an extra hundred kay that he was gonna take him apart, piece by piece."

"Shit!" Gar brought his hand down his face and blew hard. The bad news had him stressed, so he took the time to light up half of a blunt. He blew smoke up into the air and tossed the lighter aside on the table, going on to pace the floor.

"What're we gonna do?" Lil Man inquired, folding his arms across his chest.

"We're gonna give'em the money and get Lil Ace back." Lafayette told him straight like that, dumping ashes into an ashtray. "My hands are tied."

"Fuck it. If that's what we gotta do to get the young nigga back then that's what we gotta do." Gar said.

"We all agree on how we're moving on this thing then?" he looked from Gar to Lil Man.

"Yeah." The little nigga nodded.

And that was that.

Chapter 11

THE NEXT NIGHT

Lafayette was sitting on the couch watching The Dave Chappelle Show. Though his glassy, red eyes were focused on the flat-screen his mind was somewhere else all together. He was thinking about the problems he was accumulating since reaching boss status. He never had to worry about these types of issues when he was small time, going hand to hand for a few dollars here and there. Cats let him eat peacefully. The problem was he was barely scraping by. Hell, he barely had enough to feed his team, and then it only consisted of Lil Man and Gar. Now he had a clique that was fifteen workers deep. He had two cooks, four lookouts, four slingers, four gunners and two trap managers. His empire seemed to have grown over night. He began to believe that the saying was true "Heavy is the head that wears the crown."

KNOCK! KNOCK! KNOCK! KNOCK!

The rapping at the door snatched Lafayette away from his thoughts. He sat his glass of Hennessy on the coffee-table and snatched up his 17 shot .9mm before proceeding to the door. "Who is it?" he yelled out as he approached. Once the person on the other side identified themselves, he unlocked the door and unchained it. He snatched the door open and someone in a grey hoodie and dark shades crossed the threshold. Lafayette closed and locked the door behind his guest. When he turned around his guest removed their dark shades and pulled the hood from off their head, revealing their identity. It was Montrice. She smiled, exposing dimpled cheeks and a set of pearly white teeth. She grabbed the bulge in Lafayette's jeans and he grunted. She forced him up against the wall and gently bit down on his bottom lip, pulling it softly before she kissed him. She could taste the Hennessy on his breath but it didn't bother her. She wanted him in the worse way. She was a lioness and she couldn't wait to sink her fangs and claws into him.

Montrice dipped her hand into Lafayette's jeans and began to slowly massage his thickness. She started placing hickeys on his neck as she brought him to an erection. He leant his head against the wall, closing his eyes and biting down on his inner jaw. He enjoyed the sensation her touch brought him, it made him horny as hell. He was just about to crack for the ass when he came to his senses. That's when he grabbed the wrist of the hand she had down his jeans and pulled it out. A frown wrinkled her forehead as she stared up into his eyes with an expression that asked *What's wrong?*

"Relax. I got some shit I gotta handle tonight." He told her seriously.

"Oooooo, my bad."

"You got that for me?" Lafayette asked, staring down at the shopping mall bag in her hand, figuring its contents was what he had asked her for. Montrice gave him the bag and he peeked inside, the sight brought a grin to his face. It was sixty-five thousand dollars. The last of the money he needed to pay Garza off. Montrice had come through when it was crunch time. She didn't even ask him what he needed the money for. If he knew he could get her to drop this kind of loot in his lap he would have been making her break bread. Lafayette switched hands with the shopping mall bag and pulled Montrice close. "Thanks. I appreciate this."

"How about you show me your appreciation tomorrow night?" Montrice smiled. She was so close that he could fill the warmth of her breath disturb the stubble above his top lip. Her breath smelled like Big Red gum.

"You got that." He agreed, kissing her lips twice.

"Let me get up outta her before my husband stirs awake." Montrice slipped the dark shades back on and pulled the hood back over her head. She then pulled the door open and left.

***

Jason held the cordless telephone to his ear with his shoulder, while his hands were busy fixing a subway sandwich with the works. Jason was an honest hard working man who pulled sixty hours a week at his law firm. Homie was a criminal attorney; some may argue that he was one of the best in the country. Although he was a square, he had ties to the Russian mafia, often working for them whenever he was called upon.

Jason stood six foot one. He had an athletic physique and yellow skin. His hair was golden brown and cut into a fade, swirling with deep waves. Prescription eye-glasses decorated his face, making him look sophisticated and humbled. But his muscles warned knuckleheads that they may want to think twice about bumping heads with him.

"I don't know, ma. She probably went out with some friends for a couple of drinks or something. She doesn't have to tell me everywhere she's going. She's a grown woman. I'm her husband, I'm not her P.O." Jason said into the telephone as he pulled his Ralph Lauren pajama pants upon his narrow waist.

"Jason, you don't find it odd that she disappears at all times of the night?" his mother asked.

"Ma, are you insinuating that my wife is having an affair?"His brows furrowed.

"Would I be wrong for doing so? All of the signs are there, son. You've gotta open your eyes, don't play yourself. When you walk in on her on the phone, she suddenly rushes off whoever she's on the phone with. You said you guys haven't had sex in a few months, right? You don't find that a little odd? Seeing as how you said she couldn't keep her hands off of you at first?"

Jason adjusted his glasses and cut his sub down the middle with a Butcher's knife.

"Ma, I told you Montrice is insecure about her body. She's packed on a few pounds and says she doesn't feel comfortable naked in front of me. It isn't like I'd have time anyway with work and all."

"Excuses, excuses," his mother retorted, "Open your eyes, Jason Shakur."

Now Jason was pissed. Instead of disrespecting his mother, he decided to get off the phone with her.

"Ma, I'm getting sleepy. I'ma eat this sandwich and try to get some sleep. I'll give you a call tomorrow; we'll do lunch."

"Alright, love you."

"Love you, too." He hung up the cordless telephone and took a bite of his sandwich. At that moment, Montrice was coming through the door. She looked to be surprised to see that Jason was still up at that hour.

"Hey, babe," she kissed him on the lips, before picking up a sliced cucumber and taking a bite. "You couldn't sleep, huh?"

"Nope, apparently you couldn't either." He said, giving her the side eye. "I woke up hoping to fool around and you were gone. Where were you?"

"I gotta call from my sister; I had to go pick her up." Montrice lied with a straight face. "She got wasted at some bar and couldn't drive home."

"She couldn't have called her man?"

"You know that nigga Vallen aint good for nothing."

"I know it and you know it. The question is, when is she gonna wake up and realize it? This disappearing at all hours of the day and night is started to seem suspect.

I'm really starting to second guess your loyalty to me." Jason didn't let his mother know, but what she had said made a lot of sense to him. He'd just hate to believe that Montrice was stepping out on him. He'd done everything in his power to make sure his wife was satisfied in their marriage and to know that it all would have been in vain would destroy him.

"So you think that I'm getting some outside dick?" Montrice asked, hand on her hip as she wiped the Miracle Whip from the corner of his mouth with her thumb.

Jason slightly shuddered, Montrice's touch always made him weak. Even after eight years of marriage she still made his dick inflate like a balloon. "Can you blame me? As much as we used to make love. We used to do it ten times a week, now I'm lucky if it's once a month. You love sex just as much as I do, so if I'm not getting any I know someone else is." He quieted down long enough to watch her suck the Miracle Whip from her fingers, seductively.

Montrice stuck her finger into the jar of Miracle Whip and slipped it into Jason's mouth. She moaned and bit down on her bottom lip as he sucked on her finger, hungrily. Once his mouth had engulfed her finger down to the knuckle he slowly pulled away, leaving a glistening finger behind. Montrice brought her pouty lips to her husband's ear and whispered ever so gently into it. "I'm gonna take you into our bed-room…slip off my clothes…then I'm gonna fuck whatever doubts you have about us out of that handsome little head of yours. Do you understand?" Jason nodded and she slapped him so hard that it sent his glasses flyning across the kitchen; a red palm imprint was on the side of his face. Any other man would have been hot, but Montrice's assault turned him on. The nigga loved that rough shit. It made his dick hard. Licking his lips thirstily, he grabbed her by the face and kissed her deep and hard. Montrice pulled her face away, closing her eyes as he kissed and sucked on her neck.

"Uh uh, I said the bedroom." She managed to say between moans of pleasure.

"No! Fuck the bedroom!" Jason said, yanking her sweat-pants down to her knees. He slipped his Ralph Lauren pajama pants below his buttocks, exposing his hardness and snatching her up. He slammed her up against the subzero refrigerator and jammed his cock into her violently, causing her to hiss. Her eyes rolled to the back of her head. He pounded her middle as if his dick was a sword and he was trying to stab her to death. Each one of his strokes caused her head to jump up and down. Montrice's forehead was covered in sweat and her face wore a veil of blissfulness. Screams of ecstasy escaped her lips as she imagined Lafayette bringing her to a paradise of pleasure.

"Uhh! Uhh! Uhh! Uhh!" Jason gritted as he slammed him-self into his wife's pussy, his hairy buttocks moving up and down in between her juicy walls of pleasure. The veins in his dick bulged and semen oozed its way through his shaft, making his dick-head swell to twice its size. He continued to stroke her center, throwing his head back. He went faster and faster, causing her mouth to drop open and release a gasp. Homeboy was beating her shit up. She sunk her fingers into his muscular back and pulled upwards, leaving lines of blood trickling. Small fires ripped up his back and he hissed feeling them, but he continued to handle his business. "Awwww, fuck, I'm about to cum. Grrrrrrr."

"Cum for me, Daddy, bust a fat ass nut all up in my mothafucking pussy."

"Here I cum, baby!" With a grunt, he unleashed his seeds deep inside of her. At the exact moment she felt him spilling his children inside of her womb, she wrapped her thick, strong legs around him. She locked him in place where he was, as he presented her short strokes, giving her all that he had left in his nut sack. With that, he lay his hot sticky face and body against hers, breathing huskily. He then brought her down to the floor, laying the side of his face against her ample bosoms. She stared up at the kitchen's ceiling, lovingly stroking his head.

I wonder what Lafayette's doing right now, she thought.

Chapter 12

Lafayette sat in the front passenger seat watching the entrance of the establishment he was suppose to meet Garza in. It was a sleazy looking Mexican strip club that looked like it should have been shutdown a long time ago. Lafayette had driven by the place a few times, but he didn't have any idea that Garza owned the place. He thought that it must have been a front for something more criminal knowing how Garza got down.

"Is this the spot?" Gar asked as he looked beyond Lafayette at the Mexican strip club.

"Yeah, this is it." Lafayette expelled white smoke from his nose and lips. He then mashed his cigarette out in the ashtray, leaving a black streak behind. Afterwards, he fanned the white smoke from his face and told Lil Man to pass the duffle bag up front.

"You sure you don't want one of us to slide up in there with chu?" Lil Man asked, passing the duffle bag up front to his nigga.

"Nah, I'ma make this drop, get Lil Ace back, and bounce up outta there." Lafayette told him, like it was just that easy.

"Gar, keep the engine running." Gar nodded; Lafayette dapped him up and hopped out of the Regal, jogging across the street and looking both ways. Approaching the front entrance of the club, the hustler saw a shaved head Mexican in a cheap black suit watching the door. His face seemed to be stuck in a permanent scowl. Lafayette guessed it was to thwart off any knuckleheads looking to make trouble. If this was so then homeboy was in for a rude awakening. This was East L.A and you'd need more than a scowl to scare the thugs lurking in these streets.

"I'm here to see Garza." Lafayette told shaved head, switching hands with the duffle bag and brushing the imaginary lint from off of his shirt.

"Put the bag down and turn around with your arms and legs spread apart." Shaved head ordered like he rocked a badge and gun. When Lafayette assumed the position, shaved head went about the task of searching him. Once the pat down was performed he took a brief glance inside of the duffle bag. Finding that there wasn't anything suspicious inside, he handed it back to the hustler. He then opened the door and allowed him to enter. Crossing the threshold, Lafayette saw the *Open/Closed* sign turned inward on the Open side. He realized that Garza had shut the place down for their exchange. Lafayette could hear a collage of voices as he traveled down the corridor, all of them growing louder and louder the closer he drew. He took a glance inside of his duffle bag and shook his head. He couldn't believe he was about to drop $200,000 dollars into Garza's lap. A hundred bands he could live with, but $200,000? With this financial blow he was almost starting back from scratch. But he knew the exchange had to be done in order to get Lil Ace back.

Lafayette zipped the duffle bag back up as he entered the club, taking a look around. The floor was blue marble and there was tables scattered everywhere. A Mexican stripper with no ass to speak of danced provocatively on the table Garza and his three henchmen were sitting at. She shook her hips from left to right to the sound of the music, rocking the table. Glasses of alcohol spilled and caused the money that was being thrown to stick to the table top. Garza's eyes raped the stripper as her large silicone breasts moved back and forth, following the sway of her bodacious ass. He took casual pulls of his cigar and released clouds of white smoke into the air. His henchmen hooted and hollered at the stripper and kept the money flowing in abundance, dollar bills raining from everywhere.

Lafayette stood near Garza waiting to be acknowledged, but he carried on as if he wasn't there. It wasn't until the hustler cleared his throat that he finally took notice. He took the stripper by the hand and helped her down from the table, one stiletto after the other. She grabbed his dick through his tight jeans and he grunted. She pecked him on the lips and he smacked her on her pancake ass, leaving a red hand imprint behind. He watched her gather up the bills his henchmen had thrown into a clear plastic bag before turning his eyes on Lafayette.

"That's mi fedia?" he asked once he'd taken the cigar from his mouth.

"If fedia means money then, yes," Lafayette replied.

Garza held out his hand and flexed his fingers; Lafayette passed him the duffle bag. He turned to the bar where a hefty Mexican man stood cleaning out a dirty beer mug with a rag. He was balding and had fingers that resembled banana. "Cecil," he called for the bartender and snapped his fingers, motioning him forth. Having sat the mug down and threw the rag over his shoulder, the bartender lumbered over and took the duffle bag. "Be a pal and count that up for me. Will ya?" Garza snatched up a chair and smacked it down at the table. Smiling, he patted the seat of the chair and told Lafayette, "Have a seat."

"I'm good." He told him. "Just let me get the lil homie and I'm out."

"It's gonna take a while to count up that fedia, and you aren't stepping a foot outta here until I'm sure every cent is present and accounted for, so sit down." He patted the seat of the chair again. "I insist." Lafayette looked to Garza's hip and saw a .9mm automatic identical to his sitting inside of a worn brown leather holster, its strap unfastened. He blew hard and reluctantly sat down in the seat, not wanting things to go left. He looked over the three henchmen that where sitting at the table. They all had a watchful eye on him, and were either smoking squares or casually sipping liquor. Lafayette could actually feel the heat and see the steam coming from them, but he wasn't a tad bit afraid.

"So, how is business?" Garza asked.

"I don't discuss business. I'm sure you understand, being a business man yourself."

"Right, none of my business," Garza pushed a glass half filled with dark liquor in his guest's direction. "Have a drink." Lafayette picked up the glass, looked at the liquor, and then smelled it. He then narrowed his eyes into slits as he stared at the mothafucka that presented it to him.

"You poisoned this?" Lafayette kept his eyes narrowed and raised an eyebrow.

Garza laughed and said, "You must think that I'm the Devil himself. No, no poison, my friend." Lafayette shot him a look that said *'Am I supposed to believe that shit.'* Garza tossed the dark liquor from the glass onto the floor and sat the glass back down on the table top. He then filled it with Hennessy and pushed the glass over to Lafayette. "Go ahead." Lafayette picked up the glass and downed its contents. He hissed as the liquid fire swallowed his throat. When Garza went to refill his glass Lafayette looked over his shoulder. The bartender had three more stacks of bills to run through the money counting machine. Beside him there were four rows of G-stacks sitting on top of each other.

Lafayette picked up the glass of Hennessy and sipped it.

"So, how's your friend, the one missing the eye?" Garza placed a hand over his right-eye and smiled.

Lafayette clenched his jaws so tight that they pulsated. He wanted to haul off and fire on his old Mexican ass, but he knew that the cards weren't in his favor. "He's all right."

Garza looked to his henchmen and said, "You guys remember his friend, the little guy who lost his eye trying to bust Isabella's safe. He's wearing a patch now; he looks like the man on the Oakland Raiders Helmet." He laughed and the rest of his dick riding henchmen followed suit. They all cackled as if they had been told the funniest joke in the fucking world.

Lafayette's face twisted hearing Garza and his henchmen laughing at Lil Man's handicap. His top lip quivered with rage and he bared his teeth. He saw a haze of red as he looked over the henchmen and Garza's laughing faces. Everything became black and white to him and they appeared to be moving in slow motion. Lafayette could hear the growl building in his throat. He was about to take action, when he heard the Beep of the money counting machine.

That sound shot him back to reality and reminded him what he was there for. Remembering his mission, he calmed himself and took a deep breath. A strong hand gripped his shoulder; he looked and met Garza's eyes.

"I'm just busting your balls, Lafayette. I didn't take you for a sensitive guy." He patted him on the shoulder.

"If it's all the same to you, I'd like to get my lil homie and make my exit."

Garza yelled over his shoulder to the bartender, "Cecil, how much do we have there, Mano?"

"Two hundred thousand dollars," The bartender answered, placing the last G-stack on the bar top.

"The money is all there, now where is Lil Ace?" Lafayette spoke anxiously.

"Relax," Garza told him before telling his henchmen something in Spanish. The threesome rose from the table and entered the back room. When they returned they all were carrying two shopping mall bags each. They sat the shopping mall bags beside Lafayette and he looked at Garza in confusion. "Take a peek, there's nothing inside that'll bite you. I swear on The Virgin Mary." He kissed the small gold charm of The Virgin Mary that lay on his hairy chest and crossed his heart in the sign of the crucifix. Lafayette hesitantly reached into the shopping mall bag closest to his foot and pulled out something bloody and wrapped in plastic. His eyes stretched wide open when he realized that he was holding a human head. He feared that it belonged to Lil Ace but he couldn't see through the blood stained plastic. This was when he decided to rip the plastic open. Once he did this, he discovered that the head was indeed his young homie's. It held the expression of him screaming, which meant that he died in agony. Those Mexican fucks! Lafayette's eyes became glassy thinking about the pain Lil Ace experienced before having his head hacked off of his body. He was a young man that didn't get the chance to enjoy life.

Lafayette dropped Lil Ace's severed head back into the shopping mall bag. He looked up at Garza and he was staring him dead in his eyes. Garza's eyes were cold and void of sympathy. He took the cigar from his mouth and spoke, "Now I consider us even…gather your friend and get the fuck outta…" before he could finish, Lafayette snatched the .9mm automatic from the leather holster on his hip. He shot to his feet and pointed the joint at Garza's upper body.

BLOC! BLOC! BLOC! BLOC!

Garza's face twisted in unbearable pain as the hot slugs melted into his chest. The impact of the projectiles slammed him back in his chair and sent him crashing onto the linoleum, lifeless. Lafayette whipped the .9mm around and dumped two rounds each into two of the henchmen's chest. They fell back into their chairs and dropped the weapons that they'd drawn. The hustler was about to squeeze off on the third henchman when the stripper jumped on his back and clawed at his face. He hollered out and gritted. His eyes popped back open to see the third henchman pulling the trigger of his weapon. Lafayette quickly spun around, letting the stripper's back take the slugs that were meant for him. She dropped from his back and he came back around with the .9mm outstretched, blowing chunks out of the henchman's face. Bloody chunks of flesh and bone shrapnel flew everywhere.

"Aghhh," Lafayette gritted his teeth as a bullet grazed his arm. He spun around and the bartender was letting bullets fly from a small caliber pistol. The hustler let one rip through his meaty chest and a second one through his forehead. A red mist sprayed the air, hitting the dead presidents stacked upon the bar top like droplets of rain. The bartender staggered back into the shelves and knocked down bottles of alcohol before collapsing to the floor. Hearing feet running up behind him, Lafayette looked over his shoulder to see shaved head, the Mexican cat that was watching the door, charging at him. Instantly, Lafayette cracked off two more shots. The first one whizzed through his left-eye and exploded out the back of his cranium. The second one went through his cheekbone. Shaved head made a loud thud when he hit the floor. A pool of blood quickly expanded around his head, outlining it.

Lafayette ripped the shirt sleeve off one of the dead henchmen and tied it around his wounded arm. He then rushed over to the bar and began tossing the blood stained money into the duffle bag. He zipped up the duffle bag and snatched it up by its straps. Afterwards, he turned around and his heart dropped into the pit of his stomach. Garza was gone. There were droplets of blood in the space he once laid. Lafayette followed the blood droplets and they formed a trail that led to the back exit door. He ran towards the back exit door and kicked it open with all of his might. The impact from the brute force caused the door to deflect off of the wall inside of the alley. He ran down the dark path following the blood trail until it disappeared at the end of the alley. Suddenly, a primered car came to a screeching halt outside of the alley. Lafayette pointed his banger at the vehicle, but his finger froze on the trigger when he saw that it was Lil Man in his Regal.

"Did you see old boy run through here?" Lafayette inquired.

"Who?"

"Garza."

"Nah, I didn't see anybody. Get in the car, we've gotta get ghost." Lil Man said, hearing police car sirens approaching.

"Fuck!" Lafayette punched the back of the front passenger seat.

"You got shot?" Gar asked as he looked over into the backseat.

"Nah, my arm got grazed."

"What happened with Lil Ace?" Gar asked.

Lafayette shook his head. "They chopped him up and left his body parts in different shopping bags. They fucking killed him, man. They fucking killed my lil nigga." His eyes became glassy thinking about the young life that had been stolen.

Hearing the news, Lil Man and Gar shook their heads and crossed themselves in the sign of the crucifix.

Gar brought his hand down his face and blew hard. "Fuck happened in there, bruh?"

"I saw what they did to Lil Ace and I lost it. I went ham." Lafayette confessed. "I spanked the whole club. I shot Garza's mark ass like four times, but he got away."

"That's a problem." Lil Man spoke his mind. "If he's still alive then he's gonna cause one hell of a stink once he's healed up."

"Fuck'em! He can get dealt with like anybody else, ain't 'nan nigga out here bulletproof." Lafayette laid his head back against the upholstery and closed his eyes as the car coasted through the city streets.

MEANWHILE

Garza staggered into the Seven Eleven parking lot, holding his leaking chest and dripping blood along the way. He moved past a white Camero, pressing his bloody hand on its hood for leverage. When he stepped upon the curb to enter the store and removed his hand, he left a crimson palm imprint behind. Garza pushed his way through the double doors and crashed to the floor, gasping for air. He saw the cashier run from behind the counter and approach him, as he punched numbers into a cordless telephone. He stared into the cashier's mouth as he spoke into the cordless phone. His lips seemed to be moving in slow motion, but Garza couldn't hear what he was saying. Before he knew it, his vision went from blurred to black before he was lost to the world.

Chapter 13

THE NEXT DAY

"This nigga, man," Lafayette complained before redialing Shameek for the fifth time. He'd been trying to get in contact with him for the past few days, but he hadn't returned any of his calls. He needed to re-up fast.

"What's up?" Gar asked, coming through the door.

"I've been banging Shameek's line all day and he's not picking up. Shit!" Lafayette said, getting the voicemail of Shameek's cell phone once again. He ended the call and slipped the cellular into his pocket.

"You think he got pinched?"

"Hell, I hope not. I don't know anyone else with pies. At least not no good shit." He admitted.

"I can hit Gangsta up if you want; he's got some A-1 shit."

Lafayette shook his head and wiped his mouth with the back of his hand. "Gangsta letting 'em go for the forty and I hear they're stepped on. Meek's shit is pure and I get 'em for thirty. That's what? A ten rack difference? No thank you. I think I'll stay where the love is."

"Aye, I ain't mad at cha."

"Fuck it. I know where he lives. I'ma slide out to his spot. If I know Meek he isn't gonna be feeling that, but fuck'em. Niggaz gotta eat. Come on." He scooped up his car-keys and headed for the door, Gar following closely behind.

***

Lafayette crept to Shameek's front-door. He raised his fist to knock when he noticed the door was cracked open. His brows furrowed wondering why the kingpin would leave his front-door open. Figuring that someone had just left the door unlocked by accident; he pushed the thought to the back of his mind and entered the house.

"Yo, Meek," Lafayette called out as he wandered throughout the house, head on a swivel. "It's La! You left your front-door open, you're slipping, baby! You tryna be a jack-boy's wet dream or what? Yo, Meek, are you home?"Lafayette continued down the hall, checking in different bedrooms as he came across them. Passing the opened bathroom door, he thought he caught something in his peripheral so he turned around. When he stepped inside he discovered Gemma's body inside of a tub of sudsy red water. There was a gaping hole at the center of her forehead, her eyes were bugged and her mouth was wide open. Her brain's fragments were floating on the surface of the water. You could tell that she'd been screaming in terror before she was shot.

Seeing the young white girl stretched out like that put Lafayette on high alert. He pulled out his joint and proceeded through the rest of the house with caution. He didn't know if someone was still inside of the house, but he wasn't taking any chances. Lafayette followed a smear of blood on the wall that led him into the master bedroom. When he entered the master bedroom he saw that the closet light was on. He hesitantly approached the closet and peeked around the corner. Figuring that the coast was clear, he went ahead and walked inside. Clothes and shoes were strewn everywhere, and drawers were pulled out of the dressers inside of the walk-in closet. Though there wasn't any trace of Shameek's body, Lafayette figured that he was more than likely dead. It didn't take a rocket scientist to realize that his plug and his lady were the victims of a home invasion and robbery. Lafayette reasoned that they were probably killed because Shameek wouldn't give up what he had. The kingpin was stubborn as hell and would die before he let anyone take a nickel from him.

Remembering where homie kept his secret stash hidden, Lafayette jetted out of the walk-in closet. If he could get his hands on those eight blocks of cocaine he could have shit on smash, though it would be in poor taste to steal from a dead man. The hustler reasoned that Shameek couldn't take the work with him in death so he may as well take advantage of the situation.

Lafayette entered the pantry hoping and praying that the stash spot hadn't been hit. He pushed the box of Honey Nut Cheerios aside and flipped the silver switch. The back wall inside of the pantry slid upward into the ceiling and there were four blocks of cocaine left. The stash spot was four blocks shy but Lafayette wasn't tripping off of it. He was grateful for the blessing. He licked his lips and rubbed his hands together greedily, feasting his eyes on the four blocks of cocaine.

Lafayette ransacked the walk-in closet until he came up with a Louie Vuitton suitcase. Once he'd secured the four blocks of cocaine inside of the suitcase he ran out into the backyard. He tossed the suitcase over the wall and climbed over it. Landing on his bending knees, he picked the suitcase up and jogged across the street to an Arco gas station. He stopped at a telephone booth outside of the store and picked up the receiver. He dialed 911 and told them that he'd heard screams and gunshots coming from his next door neighbor's house. He then gave the operator Shameek's address and hung up. He placed the suitcase into the trunk of his Regal and hopped into the front passenger seat.

"Let's get up outta here." Lafayette told Gar, breathing hard, chest rising and falling. He looked up and down the block to see if anyone had been watching him. There wasn't anyone in sight.

Gar fired up the engine and pulled out of the Arco gas station.

"So what's up, fam?" Gar asked his right-hand man, looking to and from the windshield.

"What's up with what?"

"Meek. Fuck you think, nigga?"

"Meek is dead."

"Dead?" Gar frowned.

"Yeah, dead," Lafayette said like it was nothing. He then cupped his hand around a cigarette and sparked it up. Letting the window down, he blew out a cloud of smoke and watched the scenery as he was driven. From here on out his life would never be the same.

***

"So both of'em were laid out in there dead?" Gar asked, massaging his chin.

"His girl fa sho' got the business, I didn't see him in there but it's safe to say he's taking a dirt nap." Lafayette told him. "His place looked like The Boys raided it. I guess they were pissed off that they didn't score so they killed the girl and took him." He shook his head thinking about how his mentor's lady had been done. "We came up, though." He pulled the Louie

Vuitton suitcase closer and popped its locks. He raised the lid and revealed the four birds of raw inside. Gar smiled and picked one of the squares up, staring at it as if it was his first born.

"Man, how the fuck did they miss these?" Gar inquired.

"They were stashed inside the wall in the pantry. I saw them there the first time I copped from Meek." Lafayette relayed.

"Blood, you done came up."

"Nah, we," Lafayette motioned a finger between the two of them, "done came up."

"Fa' sho'," He sat the square back inside of the suitcase.

"I want chu to slide two of them bitches to Auntie and the other two to Diana."

Gar nodded and replied, "I'm on it, boss," before closing and locking the suitcase, picking it up from the coffee-table. He slapped hands with Lafayette and made a beeline for the door. Lafayette calling his name made him turn around with both brows raised.

"Let's make this money and not let it make us."

"All day," Gar dapped him up and strolled on out of the door.

Watch out world, here they come.

Chapter 14

Lafayette, Gar and Lil Man watched the proceedings of Lil Ace's funeral from behind the dark tinted windows of his Buick Regal. Though he wanted to make an appearance at the young nigga'z burial, he didn't want to ruffle the boy's family's feathers. He'd heard through the ghetto grapevine that his people felt that it was his fault that the youngster was dead. They reasoned that if Lafayette didn't have him in the streets hustling that he wouldn't have been kidnapped and butchered. Lafayette didn't want to kick up any drama so he just played the background. Still, he put up the bread for Lil Ace's funeral through a mutual friend of the family. Acknowledging that the boy's grandmother wouldn't accept his drug money, he had the mutual friend tell her that they'd raised the money through dinner sales and car washes.

"That's fucked up that Lil Ace's people didn't want chu at his funeral." Lil Man said from the backseat, where he was pouring Remy Martin into a clear plastic cup of ice.

Lafayette shrugged. "I ain't stunting it. Y'all didn't have to miss the lil homie's funeral on the account of me, though. They aren't fucking with me but ya'll good."

"Nah, La, fuck them." A drunken Gar waved the decease's family off. "If they don't fuck with you then they don't fuck with none of us, straight like that."

"Church," Lil Man said before taking a sip from his cup.

"They're placing the blame on you when they need to be holding the weight." Gar continued. "Maybe if they were taking care of the lil homie he wouldn't have been out in the streets with the rest of us degenerates tryna get it. You feel me?" he took a sip from his plastic cup. "I'm sorry that the homie's dead, but his death isn't heavy on my soul, and it shouldn't be on yours either, my nigga. I told the lil nigga before we put'em down that this here is grown man B.I. Shit can be going right one minute and left the next. This game ain't got no love. She's a deceitful bitch. That's why you've gotta fuck her and get on; I told'em just like that, La. And with that, the lil nigga still jumped off the porch. My soul is as light as a feather. We all make our beds and lay in 'em." He took another sip of Remy.

Lafayette blew hard before he spoke, "It's like you said, lil dude was made aware of the hazards that come with this shit before he got down. But from now on, as a rule, we don't put anyone on that's not at least eighteen. That way I can sleep at night, all right?" he looked from Gar to Lil Man.

"All right." Lil Man agreed.

"Two sho'," Gar replied.

"Cool." Lafayette took a sip from his cup.

***

The sky had turned a grayish blue and rain fell at a hundred miles an hour, hitting the street creating its own music. Lafayette rolled through the city streets with his windshield wipers sweeping back and forth across the glass, rapidly. As quick as the raindrops crashed against the windshield they were wiped away and replaced with fresh ones. Lafayette, Gar and Lil Man were all fucked up off of liquor. In fact, it was a miracle that the hustler could focus well enough to drive. He'd spent the earlier part of the day, much like Gar and Lil Man, punishing his liver with cups of Remy Martin. As of now they were headed to the nearest gas station to grab another bottle of something for the night.

Lafayette pulled into a Chevron gas station and parked at pump six. Hopping out of the car, he heard a tire explode. He looked over his shoulder and saw a stretch Lincoln Town Car pulling over beside the curb. Lafayette watched as the driver hopped out and headed to the trunk. He pulled out a spare tire and a mini jack. Taking note of this, Lafayette opened his umbrella and continued on into the gas station. Moments later, he emerged out of the gas station chewing on a red Vine and holding something inside of a brown paper bag. Lafayette reached inside of the window and sat the bag in the driver seat. He slipped the gas nozzle into the gas tank and as he pumped, he watched the driver struggle to change the tire. Every time he'd crank the limo up, the mini jack would collapse under the weight of it. Once he was done pumping gas, Lafayette screwed the cap on the gas tank and stuck the nozzle back into its slot. He then grabbed a heftier jack from his trunk and advanced in the driver's direction. Approaching the driver, he saw him pull out his cell phone and flip it open. He was punching numbers into the device when he spotted the hustler walking up.

"What's up, chief, you need a hand here?" a concerned Lafayette asked, looking from the blown tire to the driver.

"Yeah, I caught a blow out." The driver answered before sticking his cellular back inside of his suit's jacket. "I tried to crank it up, but this jack of mine isn't worth a damn."

"Help yourself." Lafayette passed him the jack that he'd gotten out of his trunk. "I would knock that out for you, but as you can see I'ma under the influence."

"Ah, don't worry about it," the driver waved him off, "I can take care of it."

The driver changed the tire and rose to his feet, smacking dirt from his palms.

"Thanks, man, you're a life saver. What's your name, brotha?" the driver extended his masculine hand.

"Lafayette." He took the man's hand.

"Larenz, but everyone calls me Ren." The driver shook his hand. "Here, let me give you a lil something," he reached in his back pocket to pull out his wallet but Lafayette stopped him.

"Nah, don't even worry about it. We're both black. I'm just looking out for my people." Lafayette told him.

"Sho' ya right." Ren passed his jack back to him. He was heading back to his car when Ren called him back over. "Lafayette, my boss would like to thank you personally."

The hustler held up a finger for Ren to give him a minute. He then sat the jack back into the trunk and slammed it shut.

"Aye, I'm tryna get back to the crib and get fucked up. I don't have no time for you to be out here playing Good Samaritan." Gar called out of the window.

"Get your drunk ass back in the window, nigga."

"Nah, for real, La, I'm tryna get faded and X-rated."

"Gimmie a minute to see what this cat wants."

"All right, hurry up."

"Hurry these nuts." He grabbed the bulge in his pants.

Lafayette met back up with Ren and he led him to the tinted backseat window of the stretch Lincoln Town Car. The window slowly descended and revealed a vision lying against the black leather seats. She was a strikingly attractive woman who'd put you in the mind of a mature Rihanna. At forty-five, she was what most would call a cougar. But her ripe breasts and juicy thighs were more than enough to give any young chick a run for her money. She was drop dead gorgeous and the aura surrounding her was one of prestige and mystique.

"Hi, how are you doing? I'm Lafayette."

"Victoria Couture." Her jeweled hand emerged from out of the window. Lafayette couldn't help but notice the flawless diamonds that adorned her fingers and wrist. They were beautiful, but paled when compared to her beauty.

"Pleasure to meet your acquaintance, Ms. Couture," Lafayette eyed her seductively as he placed a gentle kiss upon her hand, real gentleman like.

"The pleasure is all mine." She assured him with a captivating smile. "It's nice to see that there are still some gentlemen left in this world."

"I'm the last of a dying breed." He capped with a grin.

"Is that so?" she smirked. "Well, Mr. Lafayette, I'd like to thank you for giving us a hand. You saved us the trouble of having to call for…" she was interrupted by a stretch white on white Mercedes Benz pulling up beside them. "Oh, there's my ride, excuse me." She picked up her handbag and made to get out of the limo.

"Please, allow me." Lafayette opened the door for her and took her hand, helping her to her feet. He closed the door behind her and watched as she climbed into the other limousine. The driver of the other limousine hopped behind the wheel of the limousine Ren had caught a flat in and Ren hopped behind his. "Damn, you got it like that?" he asked Victoria.

"I'm heading to a business meeting, and you know what they say about first impressions." She looked inside of her handbag and withdrew a big face Benjamin Franklin. She extended it towards him and he raised his hand, refusing to accept it.

"Please, Ms. Couture," he began, "like I told Ren, I can't accept any money. I'm just tryna do my good deed for the day. I've racked up a lengthy tab with the Lord and I intend to pay it in full."

"Tryna buy your way into heaven, huh?"

"If I can't, I'll blow the gates open and bum rush my way inside."

"You're a witty one, aren't chu?" she asked. Lafayette shrugged and grinned. "Listen, I always repay my debts, so I'd like to give you something in return for helping us out."

"Your hand in marriage would be sufficient." He countered suavely. He looked to her ring-finger and saw a tanned line around it. This caused him to raise an eyebrow.

Victoria caught him looking and hid her hand. "Oh, I'm, uh, recently divorced. Finally, got up the nerve to remove my ring and start over again."

"Broke away from the old ball and chain, huh?"

Victoria nodded yes.

"Ms. Couture, I hate to rudely interrupt, but we're late for our engagement." Ren said from the driver seat of the limousine.

"I'm sorry but I must be going. Thanks again." Victoria moved to roll up the window when Lafayette stopped her.

"About how you could repay me," Lafayette began, "how about you take me out to dinner? A real classy five star restaurant would suffice."

"Maybe."

"Maybe?" his forehead crinkled.

"Yes. Gimmie a call, and if I'm not too busy, maybe we can arrange something." She took his hand and scribbled something in his palm. When she pulled the ink-pen away he saw that there were only five numbers. His forehead wrinkled and he looked up at her.

"Wait, this is only five numbers." He informed her.

"I know," Victoria replied. "Let's see how much you're willing to work that wit of yours to see me again." She kissed her fingers tips and touched them to his cheek. The limousine then rolled off into the sun set.

Lafayette stood in the street allowing the rain to hit him. He looked into his palm and saw that the rain was beginning to wash the numbers Victoria had scribbled away. He quickly closed his palm and brought it under the shade of his umbrella. A honking horn brought his attention around to his Buick Regal. He saw Gar with his head hanging out of the window.

"Come on, nigga, let's go!" he called out.

Lafayette jogged back over to his car.

Things happen for a reason.

***

Victoria picked up a glass and dumped a couple of ice cubes into it. She then picked up a bottle of Louie the XXIII and poured it half full. She wore a smirk on her face as she casually took sips of the dark liquor. It had been twelve long years since she'd entertained a man. The moment she said "I do" at her wedding, she thought her husband would be the last man that she'd ever be with. But since their separation she had been thinking about the possibilities of meeting someone else. It felt good to know that at her age men still found her desirable. She'd constantly get hit on by men her own age, but to know that she was wanted by younger men gave her an even bigger boost in confidence. Whether Lafayette knew it or not he'd just made her day and shot her already high self esteem into outer space. Victoria couldn't wipe the smirk off of her face. She was beaming like a sixteen year old girl with a high school crush.

"Boss Lady, don't tell me the young boy got chu smitten back there." Ren smiled, staring at Victoria through the rearview mirror.

"Maybe," She took a sip from her glass. She removed a joint from a small gold case she'd taken from her handbag and fired it up. She took a pull and blew a cloud of white smoke into the air. She hoped Lafayette could pull her out of the stupor she'd been in since her alienation from her husband. She was looking to get her groove back in a major way.

Chapter 15

TWO WEEKS LATER

Lafayette came strolling out of the liquor store drinking a Yoohoo with Gar beside him. They walked through the hood shooting the shit.

"Any word on Garza?" Lafayette asked, licking the chocolate liquid from his lips.

Gar shook his head and said, "Nah, it's like that nigga disappeared into a puff of smoke. Hell, he probably went back to Mexico to figure out how he's gonna get at us. Either that or he lying up in a coffin six feet under somewhere, 'cause I done checked everywhere for old boy."

"Search harder, my nigga. I don't want any surprises coming my way. Until then, let's continue to get this paper and keep our antennas up."

"You already know."

"So, what's up on the home front with chu? I hear you and baby momma beefing like crips and bloods."

Gar leaned closer to his homeboy and said, "Quiet as it's kept; I think Batice is on that shit."

Lafayette's forehead wrinkled. "What makes you say that?"

"My stash has been coming up short, La, couple hundred here and there but I've noticed."

Lafayette shrugged and said, "So she's shaving dough off top. What chick doesn't hit her man up for a few extra dollars? It's expected."

"I hear you, and I can get over that." Gar claimed. "But you should see how she's looking nowadays. She was never a real thick breezy. She's always been petite." He shook his head shamefully. "Man, if you took a mop and stood it up, I wouldn't be able to tell the difference from it and my baby momma. As long as I've been out here serving these heads, I know what a smoker looks like." His glassy eyes twinkled with hurt.

"What chu plan to do?"

He shrugged. "I don't know, my nigga, I tried to talk her into going to rehab but she ain't tryna go. We got into a bad argument this A.M and she bounced with Lil Gar. I've been blowing her up, but the bitch been shooting me straight to voicemail.

Honestly, I've been seriously thinking about getting on some strong arm shit, like really putting this hardcore thugging on this mothafucka. I'm talking about putting that banger to her head and making her ass go to the rehabilitation center. Shit, mom's can help me take care of junior."

"On some real shit, my nigga Gar, you can do all of that but it ain't gone do no good. She has to want to get clean herself; you can't make her do nothing."

"True story," Gar nodded, "I just don't know what to do, man. I'm all outta ideas."

"Don't wet it, we'll think of something."

SCREEEEECH!

A police cruiser came to a halt in front of Lafayette and Gar, stealing their attention. A female cop hopped out and Gar broke up the block; his sneakers were hitting his ass he was running so fast. The female cop drew down on Lafayette and approached him hastily.

"Try to run like your friend and I swear I'll gun you down." She barked behind dark shades with her well toned arms, holding her weapon firmly in her grasp. All that nigga Lafayette could see were her squared jaws and the skeletal bone structure in her face, below her eye ware.

"You see me busting a move? I'm not worried about a mothafucking thang." He stood where he was taking casual sips from his Yoohoo. When he went to take another sip of his beverage the female cop slapped the bottle from his hand, sending it flying across the air. The bottle shattered on the sidewalk and scattered glass everywhere, its contents dripping off of the curb into the gutter. She forced Lafayette up against the side of the liquor store and kicked his legs apart. She patted him down, but stopped once she reached the bulge in his jeans. She grabbed it and caused him to grunt.

"What the fuck is this?" she frowned.

"My dick," Lafayette's face balled up. "What kind of cop are you?"

"Shut up!" she patted around his waistline and discovered a .9mm automatic tucked on him. "Well, what do we have here?" she smiled wickedly and stuck the handgun in Lafayette's face.

Lafayette stared at the weapon and shrugged. "That ain't mine, you just planted that on me, you dirty bitch."

She tucked the .9mm in her waistline and re-holstered her gun. She whipped out her handcuffs and cuffed Lafayette's hands behind his back. The metal bracelets bit into his wrists and caused him to grimace.

"Fuck, man, these handcuffs are too tight." He complained, brows furrowed.

"You're tough; suck that shit up, nigga." She placed him into the cruiser and slammed the door shut behind him. She pulled out her nightstick and tossed it inside; it deflected off of the door panel and landed in the front passenger seat. She slipped in behind the wheel of the police cruiser and sped off.

The police cruiser stopped at the center of an alley and the female cop hopped out, slamming the door shut. She opened the backdoor and turned Lafayette around so that his legs were out of the door.

"What's up? What's this?" Lafayette scanned his surroundings, looking worried.

"Don't get scared now, macho man." The female cop scowled. "You were popping that slick shit before, right?"

"Ain't a mothafucking thang on this planet I'm afraid of, you can bet your life on that, pig!" he said with a hard face.

SMACK!

The female cop brought her opened hand across Lafayette's face, busting his lip. He spat blood on the ground and turned a pair of hateful eyes on her.

"I done told you to shut the fuck up before! If you keep flapping your big ass lips we're gonna visit the past; circa '92. You remember Rodney King, right?" She wagged the nightstick in his face before placing it on the roof of the police cruiser. Next, she quickly unbuckled his jeans and pulled them around his ankles, along with his boxer-briefs. Lafayette silently watched her strip down to her thong. She planted her knees onto her pants and grabbed Lafayette's meat, admiring it. She harped up some spit and spat a glob on it. Afterwards, she started stroking him up and down, slowly building up speed. This is when she realized that he wasn't growing hard. The mothafucka was still limp. Still stroking his dick, she noticed that he was fighting off an erection. His eyes were squeezed shut and he'd bitten down hard on his bottom lip. "Rebel, huh? I know just what to do to break your stubborn ass." She claimed, wrapping her lips around his hardness and allowing her juicy mouth to swallow him. The struggle to restrain from getting hard registered on Lafayette's face. Once again, he tried to fight off the cop's advances. His will was strong, but eventually he was ripped from this world and thrown into one of pleasure. He moaned and tilted his head back; enjoying the ecstasy her hot, wet mouth brought him.

The female cop stood to her booted feet and wiped her mouth with the back of her hand. She pulled her thong to the side and hovered over his swollen manhood, its head oozing warm semen. Seeing this, she grabbed his black pole and slowly lowered her bald sex onto it. Little momma threw her head back and gasped, feeling the hustler's member fill her up. Her eyes flickered white and she licked her lips. Lafayette stared up at her, being able to see under her chin, her succulent breasts exposed. Next, she wrapped her arms around his neck and slammed her pussy into his length repeatedly, creating her own lather. She grunted savagely and hollered out in sexual bliss. Thick veins emerged on Lafayette's forehead and neck. His eyes rolled into the back of his head. The pussy felt good to him, real good to him. The fuck session was intense and passionate. He was lost in it. The female cop was throwing her buttocks onto Lafayette's lap so hard that the police cruiser began rocking back and forth, squeaking as it did so. Nearing her orgasm, the female cop started to scream louder and louder until she finally came. Immediately, she hopped off of her fuck-buddy's dick. She was just in time to watch it shoot a fountain of warm, white jizz into the air. Once his penis was spent, it fell off to the side and rested against his thigh. The female cop got off of Lafayette and popped the trunk, withdrawing a box of wet wipes. She cleaned herself up and then got dressed. Afterwards, she un-cuffed her suspect and allowed him to clean himself up. He then put his jeans back on.

"Christ, Montrice, you put them cuffs on extra tight." Lafayette grimaced, massaging his wrists.

"My bad, boo, I got caught up in the moment." Montrice grinned. She then looked herself over in the sun-visor mirror flap, making sure her hair was still neat. Next, she laid a Listerine strip on her tongue and closed the flap.

"We've gotta stop this." Lafayette said, looking down and buckling his belt.

"Stop what?"

"This." He motioned a finger between himself and her. "Eventually you're gonna get caught, or niggaz gone think I'm snitching."

"Oh, the little baby's worried?" She made kissy faces at him, holding the lower half of his face so tight that his lips puckered up. She then gave him a quick peck on the lips and ducked back off into the front seat.

"I'm serious. You're risking your lively hood and your marriage over some dick?" his forehead wrinkled.

"Some very *good* dick I might add. Here you go," she handed him his .9mm automatic back. "And you said it yourself, my lively hood and my marriage. You let me worry about my well being, I'ma big girl." She pulled him close by the collar of his shirt and kissed him long and hard. "I'll catch up with you later; I gotta get back on duty." She slammed the door of the police cruiser.

"Hold up." Lafayette walked upon the driver side door and stooped down into the window, meeting Montrice at eye level. "I need you to check out this nigga for me."

"Who is he?" she narrowed her eyes.

"Garza Sanchez. He's the underboss of The Sanchez Cartel. His brother, Carlos Sanchez, is the head honcho."

Montrice whistled and said, "I've heard of them, those are a couple of eses you wouldn't wanna fuck with."

"Yeah, I know. That's why I'm tryna put the love on this mothafucka before he does me. I tagged his ass pretty bad. I gave'em four to the chest, but I'm not sure if he's dead. The mothafucka should be laid up in the 'spital somewhere. Any info you can get on'em would be a big help."

"Well, what chu gone give me?" Montrice ogled his packaged and then licked her lips, seductively.

"A night to remember," He smiled.

Montrice curled and uncurled her finger, signaling for him to come closer. He stuck his head into the window and she kissed him, slipping in a little tongue. "You got yourself a deal."She fired up the engine and pulled off.

Lafayette watched the back of the police cruiser as it coasted down the alley. Once it had disappeared he went on about his business.

Wherever you are, I'ma catch up with you and finish you off. You best believe that, homeboy. Lafayette thought of Garza.

Chapter 16

Loon's head lie against the thick inner thigh of a honey complexion chick that was parting and greasing his scalp to braid his hair into cornrows. Loon stood an even six feet and had an almond complexion, rocking his hair in six neat cornrows. He had a big nose and even bigger lips. He was a nigga that lived to do dirt and hustle. The mothafucka didn't know anything outside of the hood. Some would say that he was crazy, and many would agree. If homie had an issue with you, then he'd take it to the extreme to get his revenge.

Loon took casual tokes from a burning L as his thumbs worked the buttons on the PS3 controller. Four of his minions lounged inside his living room either taking advantage of the L he'd put in rotation or enjoying an alcohol beverage of their choice, while they observed the screen that had Call of Duty on display.

"Pop, pop, pop, pop, pop, pop!" Loon said, after shooting up the homie's character that he was playing against. He'd just killed him off. He slapped hands with one of his minions who were sitting near him upon the couch. "My murder game is official in these streets and in this mafucking game, act like ya know." He boasted, seeing the look of disgust on his opponent's face after he'd lost the match. "Pass the stick, ya bitch you!"

"Here, man." The losing party shoved the controller into another one of the minion's hands and rose from the seat for him to sit down.

"What chu won't on your headstone, pimp?" Loon asked, passing the L to old girl that was braiding his hair.

"Don't even try to play me, I'm not built like the rest of these niggaz you done chipped." The minion who'd just gotten the controller shot back.

"We're about to find out."

KNOCK! KNOCK! KNOCK!

"One of y'all niggaz get the door, man." Loon took the blunt from old girl that was braiding his hair.

One of the minions looked through the peephole and said, "It's your cousin, Theo and his bitch." before unlocking the door and snatching it open. Theo and Batice waltz right inside over the threshold. Theo threw his head back like 'What's up?' to some of the minions and slapped hands with the rest.

"I need to holla at chu real quick." Theo told Loon, scratching his head and then rubbing the back of it. The nigga looked like he didn't know what to do with himself.

"Yo, take care of my cousin for me; I'm tryna run this game." Loon said to the minion sitting closest to him. The minion was about to rise to his feet when Theo spoke up.

"Nah, I need to holla at chu 'bout something."

"Speak on it, cuz, we're all family here."

"My business ain't for everybody's ears."

Loon blew hard and rolled his eyes. He pressed pause on the game, took one last pull from the blunt and passed it off before getting to his feet. He motioned for his relative to follow him into the bedroom as he walked past him; Batice stayed behind in the living room where she was sized up by Loon's minions.

Loon closed the bedroom door behind Theo once he'd stepped through the door. He turned to Theo and said, "What's cracking?" he threw his head back.

"A nigga shorter than a midget on his knees, can you look out for me?"

"Nah," He shook his head, "I done looked out enough, and you still haven't hit me off with that paper like you said you were."

"I know, cousin, I know. I'm fucked up right now though. I lost my job, and Erica's been breathing down my back about this child support." Theo ran his sob story. "I just need a lil something to get my mind right, you feel me?" he scratched his under his chin and looked around bug eyed and shit. This caused Loon to frown. It was then that he took notice of his cousin's different in appearance. He looked ashy and had gotten considerably smaller since the last time he'd seen him, which was about a week ago. Homie shook his head, realizing that crack had finally gotten the upper hand on his relative.

"Theo you look like shit smeared over a saltine cracker. What the fuck has happened to you? You done fell off, loc." Loon told him straight up.

"Stall me out this one last time, Loon, we're family, bruh." Theo tightened the belt on his oversized jeans. He used to fit in them just fine, but then that monkey got on his back. Homeboy shrunk from a size 42 to a 34. He had to stab holes into his leather belt so he could tighten it around his waistline.

"Don't hit me with that family shit, tryna make a nigga feel some type of way." Loon massaged his chin as he thought about something. "Old girl in there…is that the same chick you took that ass whipping behind?"

Theo nodded and said, "Yeah, that's her."

"You still ain't gotta 'nough, huh?" he shook his head, looking at his cousin like *'You're a hardheaded mothafucka'.*

"Look, Man, if you're gonna give me shit, I'll just bounce and gone about my business." He moved for the door, but his big cousin placed a hand to his chest, stopping him in his tracks.

"Hold up. maybe, uh, maybe we can work something out."

"What chu got in mind?"

"The homie C-Bo just came home off four and a half. Let him do his thang with lil momma and I'll break you off."

"How much?" Theo asked, a hungry look in his eyes.

Loon thought on it for a second, rubbing his hands together. "I'll slide you a hunnit, but she gotta top my nigga off, too." He looked him dead in his eyes, as he continued to rub his hands together.

"All right, I gotta holla at her first, see what she says. Tell her to come in here."

"Cool." Loon smiled and left the bedroom, shutting the door behind him. A moment later Batice entered the bedroom. She was wearing a tattered burgundy wig and cheap liquor store shades.

"What's up?" she asked, chewing gum and twirling her finger in her synthetic hair.

"Listen, baby, ummm, my kinfolk is looking to get paid, he's not gone show us no love this go around."

"Well, I've only got like three dollars." She admitted, reaching her hand inside of her bra for the folded bills she had.

"Yeah, I know, and I'm broke as a joke." Theo patted his pockets. "But look, he's willing to throw us a lil something if you get down with one of his partners."

"Nigga, what?" she frowned and took her hand from out of her bra.

Batice and Theo went back and forth for about five minutes before she eventually gave in. She requested a hit of something before she got the party started. It wasn't that she needed to get high to get past what she was about to do, because she'd slept with guys for next to nothing. She just wanted to beam up because she'd been craving a blast all day.

Batice sat on the edge of the bed holding the flame of her Bic lighter under the end of her glass stem. She sucked on the end of the stem drawing smoke into her mouth and letting it circle around inside of her lungs. She closed her eyes and held the white smoke hostage before releasing it into the air. She continued to do this until she'd smoked up what was left inside of the stem.

"All right, I'm ready!" she called out to homeboy who was waiting impatiently outside of the door. At that moment, the door opened and in stepped a dark skinned brother with a muscular build. He was wearing a Du-rag and an ugly shirt decorated with palm trees, which was opened to his dingy wife-beater. Batice watched as he unbuckled his belt and slipped off his jean shorts, along with his boxers. He stood at the door long enough for her to take in his nakedness. His pubic hairs were unkempt, but below it was one of the longest and thickest cocks she'd ever seen. Her eyes bugged and she swallowed the lump of nervousness that had formed inside of her throat. Homie's penis grew harder and harder as he stepped in her direction.

Batice disrobed to her bra and panties. Du-rag helped her slip off her panties and she removed her bra herself. She looked up and his cock was staring her dead in the face, shaft full of veins and head throbbing. She spat a glob of saliva in her palm and jerked him off a bit. She then took a sip of the glass of Gin and juice on the dresser and stepped to what she was being paid for. Du-rag's eyes narrowed into slits and his big lips parted, unleashing a moan. He gripped the back of Batice's neck as she gave him a shot of head that had nearly every nigga in the Low Bottoms talking. Her mouth and tongue felt like wet, warm velvet against the skin of his joint. Du-rag found himself drooling at the mouth and moaning like a mentally challenged kid. Without realizing it, he was fucking Batice's throat, with long powerful thrust; surprisingly she didn't gag. When he felt himself about to pop, he withdrew his hard meat slowly from her mouth, inch by inch. Once it had gotten to her bottom lip it fell out, but still stood strong. Du-rag's swipe looked like a black baseball bat that had been lubricated with baby oil. This was due to its glistening.

Du-rag tore open the gold foil of a Magnum condom. He slipped it on and rolled it down as far as his girth would allow before motioning for Batice to lie on her back.

"Hold on, Centaur, I'm gonna need some lube before you go dropping all of that off in me," she placed her hand against his rock hard abs as he carried his steel to her waiting vagina. She removed a small bottle of Johnson & Johnson's baby lotion from her purse and squeezed some into her palm. She sat the bottle on the dresser and rubbed her hands together. Afterwards, she greased Du-rag's grown man up with it. She then laid back and motioned him between her legs. Homie licked his lips and crawled over to Batice. He supported his weight above her with one hand and used the other to guide himself inside of her pink tomb. Her face slowly manifested into an expression of agony, with each inch he crept up inside of her. Before she knew it, her mouth had dropped open and she'd sunk her nails into his toned buttocks. Once Du-rag had planted himself within the depths of her, he didn't waste any time pounding away at her flesh. The nigga was trying to release that four and half years worth of semen he had clogging his pipe.

While Loon and Theo were playing Call of Duty, the minions were in the hall outside of the bedroom door. They had their ears pressed against it listening in as Batice screamed in pleasure and pain as Du-rag dug her out. One of the minions licked his lips. He had his hand stuffed down the front of his jeans and was stroking his dick. The other two were on hard and could barely contain themselves from knocking down the bedroom door. All of their mothafucking asses wanted to run up in Batice.

About twenty minutes later Du-rag came out of the bedroom, pulling the door closed behind him. He was sweating immensely and zipping up his jeans.

"So what's up? Is that shit fire or what?" one of the minions asked.

Du-rag pulled off his du-rag and said, breathing hard, "Oh, yeah, shit most definitely that fire," he wiped his sweaty forehead with his du-rag and headed for the living room. "Excuse me, gentlemen."

"Man, fuck that, I'm tryna see what's that hitting for." The tallest of the minions said to his homies.

"See what's up. If we throw her a lil something, she may let us all fuck." A minion with a big head and receding hairline rubbed his hands together.

Batice was sitting on the edge of the bed slipping her sandals back on when the bedroom door opened. Loon stepped in clutching two sandwich bags with off white crack rocks in them. Batice was so focused on the rocks that she didn't even hear what he was saying to her. Her eyes were as big as gulf balls and she licked her lips. It wasn't until Loon gripped her shoulder and looked into her eyes that she snapped out of her trance.

"Aye, you hear what I said?" he asked, wondering where the hell her mind was.

"My bad, what chu say?" she looked up at him, making eye contact.

"I said, 'here's your payment for knocking off the homie.'" he sat one of the bags of crack on her lap. "I was saying that I'd hit chu off with double that if you'd take care of me and the rest of my niggaz." He held up the other bag of crack. The bag was pinched between his fingers. He swung it back and forth, trying to put her under its hypnosis. It worked too. Her smoked out ass was following every sway of the bag of rocks. The rocks inside of this bag were twice the size of the ones inside of the other. Though the rocks were bigger they were less potent than the others. This was because their maker was heavy on the bacon soda. A lot of D-boys did this to make crackheads think that they were getting more bang for their buck. It was an old strategy, but it worked on green smokers like Theo and Batice.

Batice licked her lips again. She looked from the bag in her hand to the one pinched between Loon's fingers and her greed got the best of her. She wanted them all.

"How many?" she inquired.

"Plus me? Four," He held up four fingers.

"All right," Batice nodded rapidly. She tried to grab the bag but he snatched it back from her.

"Not so fast, lil momma, you gotta handle business first." He opened the bedroom door and stuck his head out into the hall. "Y'all niggaz come on!"

The three of Loon's minions came through the door; they didn't waste any time peeling off their clothes and slipping off their underwear.

"Hold up. I thought we were doing this one at a time?"

"Nah, we're all gone go, it'll be faster this way." Seeing that Batice was thinking on it and could possibly change her mind, he decided to give her another flash of the bag. "Look, when we're done, your shit will be right her waiting for you, OK?" Batice nodded yes. She watched him drop the bag into his top nightstand drawer and close it shut.

Loon pulled off his black sweatshirt and set his gun on the nightstand beside his cell phone. He slipped off his white T-shirt and unbuckled his jeans, exposing the stubble on his mound. He watched as the tallest of his minions grabbed Batice by her legs and pulled her to the edge of the bed. He'd inserted his dick into her pussy, while another minion stuck his into her mouth. Batice stroked a third minion's hardness, while she sucked on another's. The bedroom quickly filled with the pleasured moans and groans of men, along with slurping and suction noises. Loon entered the fray, stroking his meat and ready to get his money's worth.

Theo cracked open the bedroom door and stuck his head inside. For a time he watched Loon and his minions sex Batice. Suddenly, her eyes shifted to him and they held one another's gaze. Breaking eye contact, she went back to sucking them niggaz' dicks while they took turns running up in her. Theo quietly closed the bedroom door and brought a chair into the hall, placing it just outside the bedroom door. He sat down in the chair and glanced at his watch, wondering how long it would take all of them niggaz to bust their nuts so he could get high. Figuring he'd be there for a while, he pulled a cigarette from the pack of Newports in his breast-pocket and fired it up. Leaning his head back against the wall, he casually smoked the cigarette and listened to the sounds of bliss and pain coming from out of the bedroom, where all of the fucking was going on.

TWO HOURS LATER

Hearing the bedroom door open, Theo reached down between his legs and mashed what was his fourth cigarette out into the glass ashtray. He looked back up just in time to see Loon's minions filing out of the door. Loon was the last one through the door. He came out tucking his gun on his waistline and slipping his sweatshirt back over his head. He smiled at Theo and dapped him up.

"What's up, cuz? You've been sitting out here this whole time?" Theo nodded. "Check it out, lil momma got some bomb ass pussy," he pointed a thumb over his shoulder to the bedroom, "Anytime y'all tryna get ya'll minds right, holla at cha big cousin."

"Fa' sho'," He nodded. Once Loon went on about his business, he ducked off into the bedroom. As soon as he crossed the threshold his nostrils were assaulted by hot, smelly sex. The humid, pungent air was literally suffocating him. That's when he smacked his hand over his nose and mouth, breathing the best way that he could.

Theo found Batice sitting on the edge of the bed. She had on her baby T-shirt and thong underwear. She rose off the bed, slowly putting on her zebra striped leggings, one leg at a time. Theo could see the pain on her face with each leg she slipped through the leggings.

"Are you, OK?" he asked concerned.

"My pussy is killing me. Them niggaz are hung like a bunch of donkeys." She winced, having finally pulled the leggings upon her waist. She picked up the sandwich bag of crack rocks from the dresser.

"Is that it? Where is the rest?"

"He put it in that top drawer over there." She pointed to the nightstand. Theo picked the second bag of crack up from the top nightstand drawer. He licked his lips like a hungry dog seeing the size of the rocks it held. He rolled the bag up and stuck it in the pocket inside of his jacket. "We can get as high as giraffe pussy with this."

"Help me outside to the car." Batice winced with each step she took. She slung her purse strap over her shoulder and reached for Theo. He took her by the arm and helped her through the door.

Crack cocaine is one hell of a drug.

Chapter 17

"That was my lil freak bitch I was telling you about." Lafayette told Gar. He was telling him who the female cop was that had snatched him up.

"When I saw that breezy pull your banger from your waistline, I thought for sure you were gone be gone for a minute." Gar admitted. He and Lafayette were posted up at the car wash on Florence and Hoover, watching the Mexicans as they toweled down his maroon Dodge Magnum. "I don't fuck with The Ones, my bitch or otherwise, but I can't front...having a pig on your team can work in your favor. Bitch may come in handy one day, feel me?"

Lafayette nodded. "Old girl is married to some caked up attorney. That fool cops her any and everything she wants. That's how I got my hands on them bands to get Lil Ace back; bitch dropped it in my lap, like here. Didn't ask me no questions or nothing."

"She's a keeper, huh?"

"Yeah, well, at least until I get tired of the bitch."

Gar laughed and playfully punched Lafayette in his arm. Right after his cell phone was ringing with a text message. He pulled it out of his pocket and glanced at the screen. A line etched across his forehead. "Yo, this Lil Man, he said it's going up tonight in Hollywood. You tryna hit the strip? What's up?"

"Yeah, I'll fuck with it. I need a break from the hood."

"Cool. We're on then." Gar shot a text message back to Lil Man, letting him know that they were going to turn up in Hollywood.

A black X5 pulled into the parking lot stealing Lafayette and Gar's attention. The driver side door opened and a tall, slender light skin nigga hopped out. He had caramel brown eyes and curly hair that was tapered into a fade. He looked like he belonged in a magazine modeling Calvin Klein underwear or some shit. He was so pretty that he almost looked like a woman. He pulled a folded wad of bills from his pocket and removed the gold money-clip that held it in place. He peeled of a bill and passed it to the car wash attendant. He called the attendant's attention to his tires and Lafayette assumed that he was telling him to put extra Armoral on his wheels. After talking with the attendant, the pretty boy advanced in Lafayette and Gar's direction. Once he'd gotten about ten feet they realized who he was.

"Man, that's Chill," A smirking Gar tapped Lafayette. "Old pretty ass nigga."

Chill approached Lafayette and Gar, cheesing like a mothafucka. His teeth were pearly white and looked like they belonged on the whitening chart inside of a dentist office. Chill was a get-money nigga that the fellas knew from around the way. He was a real flamboyant and flashy type of dude. He was loud and boasted a lot of paper. He made it his business to be the center of attention wherever he went.

"What's crack-a-lacking, my ninjas?" Chill slapped hands with Gar and Lafayette.

"What's up, baby boy?" Gar shot back. "I see you're out here doing your thang." He admired his X5 truck.

"Oh, that old thang?" Chill down played his SUV. "That ain't nothing, just my little weekend toy. You should see this new joint I just copped, though; milk white Audi with the peanut butter guts. I'm telling you, it's the most beautiful Caucasian bitch you'll ever see."

"Is that right?" Gar responded, still admiring the X5.

"Yeah, man, I may breeze through the hood in it one time to let chu see what I'm working with. Hell, I may let chu just have the mothafucka, I gotta 'bout ten more rides, anyway. You know me, once the year expires I turn them bitches over and go get me something new, feel me?" He fogged the face of his Presidential Rolex and polished it off on his shirt.

"Sho' you're right."

"Yo, Lafayette, I heard you got it percolating around your way, baby, let a nigga hold something." Chill turned his attention on Lafayette.

"I'm short, homie. If I had it I'd throw it down and make you take it." Lafayette capped. He wasn't about to give that nigga shit. Shit, it wasn't like he needed it anyway. That mothafucka wasn't hurting.

"Ah, nigga, come again," Chill tilted his head and gave him a look like *'Come on, now'*. "They say Baby from Cash Money Records don't got shit on you, you're the real Birdman. Cats say you deal with more bricks than a construction worker. I know you holding."

Chill's big mouth was getting Lafayette hot, but he fought to keep his cool. He picked imaginary lint from his shirt and brushed his shoulder off. "You know how most of these niggaz are…they just like to hear themselves talk. They don't know nothing about nothing. I'm just tryna get by like everybody else; holding on like a hubcap in the fast lane."

"Yeahhhh," Chill gave him the side eye, but decided to change the subject. He could see he was getting tight and didn't want to press him any further. "How is big bro doing?"

"He's all right; he'll be home in a minute."

"That's what's up."

"Aye," Gar tapped Lafayette, "she's ready." He said referring to his car, which was cleaned up and ready to go. He slapped hands with Chill and started off towards his whip. Lafayette was right behind him when Chill called after him.

"What's up?" Lafayette threw his head back.

Chill peeled off a few Benjamin Franklins and passed them to the hustler. He looked at the money then back up at its owner, wondering what it was for. "That's for big bro, tell'em Chill said, what's up?"

Lafayette nodded and tucked the money into his pocket as he turned and walked off.

***

Batice and Theo lie upon his sofa intoxicated. They'd gone through a good amount of the crack in the sandwich bags before they'd achieved the ultimate high. Batice had forgotten about her throbbing pussy and Theo had gotten over his guilt of letting his cousin and his niggaz run up in her.

"Man, almost all of this shit is gone." Batice studied the contents of the sandwich bag as she held it up.

"Yeah, fam bam fucked us, this shit was heavy on the bacon soda." Theo stated, putting the flame back to the glass stem and taking deep pulls.

"Your trifling ass cousin, I should have known something was up. Look how much we had to go through to finally get high." Batice shook her head and took the glass stem and Bic lighter from him. She fired up the glass dick and took a few drags. Batice lay back on the couch and passed the smoking utensil and Bic lighter to Theo. He took the items and lay back beside her. He was about to light up when he looked to Batice.

"Suck my dick," He said it like he was saying iron this shirt for me, but he always spoke to her ass like that.

Batice unzipped his Dickie's and pulled his meat out through the hole inside of his boxer's. She spat into her palm and used the saliva to lube up his steel. With that done, she moved to bestow her blessing upon him.

"Mmmmmm," Theo shut his eyes and a smile spread across his lips. Afterwards, he fired up the pipe and sucked on the end of it, causing smoke to waft around him. As Batice continued to suck him off, he carried on smoking.

Chapter 18

THAT NIGHT

Gar and Lafayette were kicking it inside of VIP on a black leather sectional sofa, the air was so heavy with weed smoke that it was easy to catch a contact. Thanks to Lil Man. He kept at least two blunts in rotation amongst their crew. There were five empty gold bottles of Ace of Spades on their table and one unopened one. Every time a bottle would get halfway empty Gar would order up another one. He tipped the waitress a Benjamin for every bottle she brought back to the table. He wanted the whole spot to know that his crew was in the house and they were doing big things and making major moves.

"Aye, this mothafucka live tonight." Gar told Lafayette after jumping down from the couch where he was dancing with two gold bottles of Ace of Spades in his hands to Future's *'Karate Chop'*. He sat one of the bottles on the table and used a couple of napkins to pat the beads of sweat from his forehead.

"Hell yeah, man." Lil Man replied. He'd just crossed the velvet rope of the VIP section and approached the table.

"What happened to old boy you were with a minute ago? Homie was real cool, we was chopping it up and shit."

"Oh," Lil Man leaned closer so that Gar could hear him. "I pounded it out in the Men's room and sent his ass home to get ready for the encore, feel me? Hahahahahahaha." he laughed and nudged Gar.

"Ewwwww, too much info, blood," Gar made a disgusted face.

"Where's La?" Lil Man inquired, having come down from his laughter.

Gar nodded over his shoulder, "On the couch with that yamp (young tramp)."

Lafayette was lying back on the sectional sofa with a pretty little thang on his lap, whispering in his ear and planting tender kisses on the side of his face. She was wearing a net dress, which exposed the black bra and panties she had on. Her body slightly glistened from perspiration having been dancing on the floor for the better half of the night. A mixture of sweat and a sweet fragrance invaded Lafayette's nostrils, but he didn't mind much. The young woman on his lap was sexy and made his cock stab into the material of his pants. Homie was loaded and casual sipping champagne. While his right-hand held the flute, his left-hand gently swept back and forth up the woman's thigh. He could actually feel the warmth her bald kitty expelled.

"What is that bitch? Brazilian?" Lil Man asked Gar about the nationality of the woman sitting on Lafayette's lap.

He shrugged. "Who knows, I'd fuck her though."

"You'd fuck anything."

"Ain't that about a bitch?" Gar looked at Lil Man like he had some nerve. He remembered that night that the cartel had snatched up Lil Ace. Lil Man was inside of the alley getting his dick sucked by some crackhead nigga.

"What?" Lil Man smiled. He knew exactly what Gar was getting at. Gar looked back to the dance floor, waving his the little nigga off. He wasn't about to entertain his bullshit.

Lafayette rose from the sectional, taking the Brazilian beauty by her hand. He approached Gar and Lil Man. "One of y'all niggaz got some Jimmy Hats?"

"What's up? You out?" Gar passed Lafayette a Magnum.

"Nah, I'm finna slide off to the car real quick." Lafayette took the golden square foil wrapper.

"All right, do your thang chicken wang." Gar smiled and patted his right-hand man on his shoulder; Lil Man did the same as he passed. The hustler navigated his way through the bodies crowding the dance floor with his fuck-buddy for the night in tow. Nearing the front exit, a familiar face caught his attention. He had to take a double take; he couldn't believe that it was her. Victoria Couture. She was being towed through the crowd by Ren, whose face read '*Your best option is not to fuck with me*'. He was strong arming his way through the maze of bodies and no one thought to challenge him for his rudeness. This was probably because Ren was a 6 foot 4 brother, with a physique that put you in the mind of The Rock. Lafayette stopped in his tracks and watched as Ren and Victoria disappeared inside of the crowd. He went after them in a hurry, brushing shoulders with party goers as he made his way. He was a few feet behind them when they went through the exit door. As soon as he stepped across the threshold, his head whipped from left to right. He saw Ren opening the backdoor of a stretch Mercedes Benz for Victoria. Once she went to duck her head to get inside, Lafayette turned to his Brazilian jump-off.

"Say, baby, why don't chu gone ahead and get in the car for me." He passed her his car-keys. "It's a primered Buick Regal. Hit the lil alarm there, it'll sound off."

"OK. Don't leave me waiting forever." She brought her smooth, manicured hand around his face and then pecked his lips before sashaying off to the car. Her high heels clicked on the ground as she went on about her business.

Lafayette looked to the stretch Mercedes Benz that Ren had just hopped in and closed the driver side door. He ran over to the tinted passenger side window and knocked on the black glass. The window rolled down and he was greeted by Ren's smile. It tripped Lafayette out how old boy was wearing the face of a harden convict just moments ago, and now here he was smiling like he was about to take his class picture.

"What's up, Lafayette?"

"What's cracking, Ren? I didn't know y'all were inside."

"Yeah, boss lady likes to hit a night club every now and again."

"Is that right? You think I could holla at her, real quick?"

Ren rolled the window down that would allow him to peer into the backseat. He asked Victoria about speaking with Lafayette and then he turned back to the hustler. "It's OK. Go ahead." He motioned him to the back window.

"All right, thanks, big time." Lafayette patted the roof of the stretch Mercedes Benz and moved to the back window. As he approached the back of the vehicle the window descended. At that moment he was face to face with the lovely Victoria Couture. She was just as beautiful as she was when he first laid eyes on her. Her eyes were glazed over and a smirk was plastered on her face. He could tell that she was tipsy.

"How're you doing, Miss Lady?" Lafayette greeted her with a smile.

"I'm peachy, thank you, and how about you, handsome?" she returned the gesture.

"I'm good, now that I've ran into you." He flirted. "You stole my heart that day. Now I know you didn't think you were gonna get away with what belongs to me?"

"My, my, my, don't we have a way with words." Her arms were resting on the window pane and her face was about two inches from his now.

"I'm just keeping it one thousand, beautiful."

"Is that a fact?"

"That's the truth."

"If you're so into me, Mr. Lafayette, why didn't chu figure out the last digits of my number and call me?"

"I did figure them out, I just been so busy I hadn't gotten the chance to call you."

Victoria tilted her head to the side and looked at him like *'Get out of here with that bullshit'.* Ironically, her cell phone rang and she told Lafayette to give her a minute to answer it. She frowned when she looked at the screen because she didn't know who the number belonged to. Acknowledging this, she pressed *'answer'* and placed the cell phone to her ear.

"Hello?"

"I told you I figured those numbers out." Lafayette spoke into his cellular, smiling. He then ended the call and slipped the cell phone back into his pocket. Victoria beamed brightly. She couldn't stop smiling. "So what's up? Are we going to stop doing The Tango or are you going to give me the time of day?" Victoria glanced at her gold Rolex watch, causing Lafayette to grin. "Hilarious. You should be a standup comedian."

Victoria chuckled. "I'm kidding, sweetie, but what're you going to do about your little friend you sent to the car?" Lafayette frowned. He didn't know she'd seen him pass his car-keys off to homegirl he'd planned on freaking off with in the backseat of his Regal. "You didn't think I peeped that play? I congratulate the player and respect the game."

"Say the word and she's gone." He said seriously.

"Awww," she rubbed the side of his face, "You'd do that for me?"

"It's your world, love; I just want a minute in it."

Victoria stared into Lafayette's eyes searching for deceitfulness. She didn't find any, he was sincere. Lafayette couldn't help but wonder what was going through her mind. She cleared her throat and spoke, "I'll tell you what…you go ahead and play with your friend tonight. You call me tomorrow evening and maybe then we can link up."

Lafayette stood erect as the black tinted window rolled up. He looked on as the stretch Mercedes pulled away from the curb and into the Hollywood traffic. Having seen Victoria off, he trekked across the parking lot in the direction of his car. Along the way something glowing in the shadows caught his eye. He looked over his shoulder and saw two silhouettes standing beside an old raggedy Buick LaSabre. He could feel their eyes on him, but didn't pay them any mind. He went about his business as he made his way towards his car.

"Yo, Lafayette, is that you?" one of the silhouette's spoke.

The first thing Lafayette thought was Garza had sent a couple of his men to lay claim on his life. The crunching of gravel let him know that the silhouettes were falling instep behind him. Danger alarms went off inside of his head; he dashed to the driver side door with the silhouettes chasing after him. He snatched opened the driver side door and grabbed his banger from underneath the seat. He came up out of the car and swung his heat around, ready to let somebody hold some hot shit.

"Easy, homes, we come in peace," one silhouette said with his .357 Magnum revolver and his .44 Magnum revolver pointed dead in Lafayette's face. The other silhouette was standing beside him. She had his Desert Eagle pointed at Lafayette.

"Who the fuck are we?" Lafayette mad dogged him.

"Damn, homie, you got cataracts or something? It's Zay and Chat."

Lafayette peered through the darkness and made out the faces. He was hesitant to lower his joint knowing how Zay and La'Chat got down for theirs. When they were looking for a come-up no one was off limits. They were only for themselves.

"I'll tell you what, I'ma gone and put these bad boys away so we can rap for a few ticks, cool?" Without waiting for his response, Zay stashed his revolvers on his waistline. He looked to La'Chat and she still had her joint pointed at Lafayette's face. He placed his hand on the barrel and gently pressed it down. "It's OK, baby, you can lower that thang." La'Chat did as her man ordered. "Are we good now?"

Lafayette's reply was tucking his banger in the front of his pants.

"What's up, La? Is that how you welcome your nigga home? Show your boy some love." Zay opened his arms. The hustler was hesitant at first, but he went ahead and embraced him, all the while keeping his eyes on that mothafucka's woman.

"Lafayette, do you want me to call the police?" the Brazilian jump-off asked, holding a cell phone in her hand. She wore a worried expression on her face.

"Bitch, who the fuck you plan on calling Binem on?" La'Chat scowled. She moved to put hands on the Brazilian, but Zay stretching his massive arm across her chest stopped her.

"I'm good, sweetheart." Lafayette told the Brazilian jump-off. "Matter of fact, we have to do this some other time. I need to catch up with my folks."

The Brazilian jump-off nodded and dropped her cell phone into her purse. She approached Lafayette and kissed him on the lips. "Call me, OK?" he nodded yes. The Brazilian walked off with La'Chat staring daggers at her until she was out of sight.

"So what's up, baby boy, how're you living?" Zay nudged Lafayette.

"I'm getting it how I live, like I always have. You know me."

"Still corner hustling, huh? Maybe it's time you stepped your game up."

"I'm trying; a nigga just can't seem to get right, though."

"Believe me, I know how it is." Zay took the time to light up a cigarette.

"What y'all doing posted up out here? Parking lot pimping?"

"You shouldn't even have to ask that. You already know what type of shit me and wifey be on." He flashed a wicked smile. He and La'Chat were laying low in the parking lot looking for some poor bastard to lay on for all he had. Though night clubs were notorious for fronting ass niggaz acting like they were bossed up and caked out, the couple figured they'd be lucky enough to catch a sucker slipping for a few bills.

"Right, how silly of me."

"Say, La, you've been in the mix as of late. You wouldn't happen to know of any cats that are out here handling, now would you? I'm willing to cut chu in on a third of the take. You wouldn't even have to get your hands dirty."

Lafayette pretended to think on it for a minute. He'd already made up his mind that he wasn't going to set some poor soul up to get got by Zay and La'Chat. That just wasn't how he rocked. If they robbed cats for their grips then that was their business, but he wasn't going to get involved.

"Nah, I don't know anyone that's handling that's worth your while. All the cats I know are small fish like me, but I can't hang them out to dry. They're family."

"Damn," Zay cursed, "You don't know anybody?" he raised an eyebrow.

"Nah, man," Lafayette shook his head, "But if I think of anyone, I'll get at chu."

"All right," Zay nodded and tapped his cigarette, dumping ashes. He took Lafayette's cell phone and programmed his name and number into it. He then handed it back to him. "Make sure you get at me if anything comes up. A nigga starving and I'm trying to eat, ya heard?" he made to leave but turned back around. "Oh, Lafayette, we're free agents out this bitch, big dawg, so if there are any niggaz you feel that needs that Act Right, don't hesitate to call. I don't got no problems riding down on a nigga and give'em that hammer time."

"I'll keep that in mind."

Lafayette watched as Zay and La'Chat hopped into their raggedy Celebrity and drove out of the parking lot. He turned to his right and Gar and Lil man were approaching.

"What's up, La? You good?" Gar asked.

"I'm Gucci."

"Fuck was that?" Lil Man inquired.

"Zay and La'Chat," Lafayette answered. "As soon as they find out that I'm on the rise, they'll be back."

"We'll be ready for'em." Lil Man gripped his homeboy's shoulder, letting him know that he and Gar had his back.

All for one and one for all.

Chapter 20

THE NEXT NIGHT

Lafayette stood before the mirror of the medicine cabinet shaving, frolics falling inside of the porcelain sink. With each stroke of the barber razor, he'd leave a strip of clean, damp skin behind. He'd then move the razor back and forth inside of the sink of murky water until it was free of shaving cream and hair. Once he was done, he'd tap the razor on the edge of the porcelain sink and go back to the task at hand. Tonight he was supposed to go out with Victoria Couture. He couldn't help but feel giddy inside. It wasn't like he hadn't stepped out with gorgeous women before. Shit, he'd shared company with some of the most attractive women that the city had to offer, but Ms. Couture was in a class all of her own. He couldn't put his finger on it, but it was something special about her. She had an essence surrounding her that sort of pulled you in. He couldn't help but to be drawn in. It was kind of like how a fish would be baited by a worm at the end of a hook.

Lafayette finished shaving and dried his face. He stepped into his bedroom, where he got dressed. He slipped on a cream button-down shirt, black slacks and cream slip-in Hush

Puppies. He accessorized with gold frames and a Michael Kor's watch. He gave himself a look in the full length mirror before spraying on designer cologne. He sat the bottle of cologne down on the nightstand and made for the front-door.

***

Lafayette pulled up into Victoria's cobble stoned driveway. The first thing that caught his eye was her mansion. It was tan and brown and the size of a castle. The estate put you in the medieval time's era. Lafayette got the feeling that a couple of knights in armor riding on a couple of horses were going to come galloping down the steps to dual right out front. Remembering what century he was in, Lafayette popped a stick of Winter Fresh gum into his mouth and hopped out of his rental. It was a 2013 BMW 745. It was black-on-black with stock rims. Lafayette was going to roll his Regal but he wanted Victoria to know that he wasn't just some hood nigga. He wanted her to see that he knew how to dress and conduct himself outside of the ghetto.

Lafayette looked himself over in the side-view mirror, making sure there wasn't any food in his teeth or scum in his eyes. He stood erect and adjusted the banger on his waistline. As soon as he stepped forth he heard the ferocious barks of dogs coming from his right. He looked and two Doberman Pinschers came charging at him from out of the darkness. A second pair of barks came at his rear, he turned around and two more Doberman Pinschers were coming at him. Lafayette snatched his 17 shot .9mm from his slacks. He went to lift it and ended up dropping it. He was about to pick the banger up when he saw one of the dogs leaping forth. Lafayette cracked the dog in the jaw and kicked another one in the neck. He dove to the lawn, scooping the banger into his hands. He turned around and one of the dogs had its mouth open about to bite him. Lafayette held up his arm to guard his face from the beast's fangs and closed his eyes. He heard someone snap their fingers. He waited for the fangs to sink into his arm but they never came. His eyes peeled open and he looked around. The dogs were standing on either side of him, panting with their tongues hanging out of their mouths. The violent intent had vanished from their eyes. They seemed humbled and disciplined. Lafayette looked to the porch of the mansion and Ren was there. He walked down the steps and onto the lawn. He snapped his fingers once more and the Doberman Pinschers dispersed, back into the darkness from where they came.

Ren approached Lafayette and extended his hand. The hustler grasped it and the big man pulled him upon his feet.

"Are you, OK?" Ren asked. Lafayette nodded. "Sorry about the dogs. I meant to put them up before you came but it slipped my mind."

"It's cool, don't worry about it." Lafayette panted, stashing his banger back into his waistline. He brushed the grass from off his shirt and saw that he had green stains in it. "Shit. This a three hundred dollar shirt."

"If you give me that shirt, I'll have it dry cleaned for you. You can borrow one of mine for the time being."

"Good looking out." He slapped hands with Ren.

"Come. Follow me." Ren motioned for him to follow him inside of the mansion.

When Lafayette stepped inside of the mansion he noticed its 17th Century décor. The chocolate marble floors were buffed so shiny that you could see your reflection in it. Its ceiling was as high as the one inside of the Taj Mahal. The ceiling had a painting on it of a red horned demon leading an army of bat-winged demons into battle against an angel carrying a huge sword, who was leading an army of sword toting angels. The painting was beautiful. It looked like the artists that painted the ceiling of the Sistine Chapel had painted it. Lafayette was in wow of the enormous resident. One could easily get lost inside of it if he didn't know its layout like the back of his hand.

Once Ren had given Lafayette a shirt, he led him to Victoria's bedroom door. He knocked on the door and heard her holler for him to come in. Lafayette opened the door and stepped inside, looking around. The boss lady had an oak wood canopy bed. Its mattress was covered by a beige comforter and about ten pillows in different shapes and sizes. Against the wall on the side of the bed was a suede chocolate love seat and at the foot of the bed there was a worn, rusting brown treasure chest. Beyond the bed, mounted on the wall, there was a "70 flat-screen television.

"Victoria?" Lafayette called out, head on a swivel.

"I'm in here, sweetie." Victoria called out from behind the bathroom door. Taking note of where her voice had come from, Lafayette opened the door and stepped inside. He looked away once he saw her lying inside of a Jacuzzi size bathtub at the center of the bathroom. Her nakedness was covered in soap suds and steam was rising from the hot water. The temperature from the hot water made her face and the rest of her shiny.

"Come on in." she said, sipping her glass of red wine. Her long hair was pinned up in a bun to keep the water from wetting it.

"I can wait out in the bedroom, if you'd like."

"Nonsense, come right in, I'm sure I don't have anything you haven't seen before on a woman; slightly aged of course, but the same nonetheless." She presented him with a smirk. "Have a seat," she motioned towards the antique chair sitting at the vanity. Lafayette sat the chair not too far from the in-floor Jacuzzi size bathtub and sat down. "Would you like something to drink?"

"Sure, I could go for a lil taste of something."

"Help yourself." She gestured towards the empty wine glass and the expensive bottle of red wine.

Once Lafayette poured himself a glass of red wine, he took the time to admire the décor of the bathroom. "This is a nice place you have here. If you don't mind me asking, what do you do to afford a place like this?"

"Don't ask me any questions and I won't tell you any lies." She swirled the wine around inside of the glass.

"Secrets, huh? Now I'm curious."

"Remember, it was curiosity that killed the cat."

"Aye, you can't kill a nigga for being curious." He smiled.

"Oh, yes I can." She made her hand into the shape of a gun and pointed at him. As foam dripped from it, she said, "Bang! You're dead!" Silence fell between them. She took a sip of wine and looked back to him. He was staring and grinning at her. She blushed. "What?"

"You are one fine ass mothafucka. I mean that shit, too. You're ass is drop dead gorgeous, for real, for real. I don't know who your husband is, but he's gotta be kicking himself in the ass for leaving you."

Victoria blushed just that much more, her cheeks turning rose petal red. "I must say that you've made my night with that compliment. It's nice to hear that someone so young finds me attractive and desirable, especially with me getting up there in age."

"Age ain't nothing but a mind state." Lafayette said, putting his finger to his temple. "See, you're only as old as you think you are. How old do you think you are?"

Victoria thought on it for a moment and then said, "Twenty-five."

"You're twenty-five and I'm forty-five. If cats see me out in the streets with you they're gonna be like 'Aye, man, how that old dude pull that sexy ass twenty-five year old? I bet he either gotta big dick or Bill Gates' bank account. If not, both.'"

Victoria busted up laughing, spitting red wine everywhere. Some of the wine squirted out of her nostrils and she covered her nose with her hand. "I'm sorry, but you are just too funny."

"Here," he passed her a washcloth, watching her wipe the wine from her face.

"So what do I have to look forward to in our little date tonight?" she asked.

"Well, I thought we'd start off with dinner at this Italian restaurant and then…"

"Boring, boring, boring," Victoria cut him off as she swirled her wine around inside of her glass. "The dinner and the movie thing: been there and done that. Why don't we kickback here, stuff our faces with chili cheese dogs, root beer floats and watch 80s action flicks? Afterwards, we can cap the night off with a little, I don't know…fucking…" she turned her eyes on Lafayette as she sipped wine. He damn near choked on the red wine, scooting his chair back so he wouldn't spill any on his shirt.

"Yeah, uh, we can do that." Lafayette wiped his mouth with the back of his fist.

"Shit." She sat her glass down beside the tub and rubbed her eye.

"What's up?"

"I got something in my eye, could you blow it for me?"

Lafayette sat his glass of wine down on the vanity and approached Victoria. He kneeled down to her and said, "Let me see your eye." he went to blow into her eye and she pulled him into the water. She forced him up against the tub, kissing him hard and passionately.

Victoria ripped open Lafayette's shirt, sending buttons flying everywhere.

"Damn, this is Ren's shirt." He told her.

"I'll buy him a new one." She gasped, helping Lafayette remove his shirt and then his wife-beater. Next, his slacks and boxer-briefs were thrown out of the water. He lifted Victoria up, carried her out of the tub and laid her on her back. He slipped his wet dick into her shaved vagina and proceeded to fuck her on the wet marble floor. The two of them went at it like a couple of college kids. In those twenty minutes, Victoria was transported back to when she was nineteen years old and had indulged in the greatest sex of her life.

***

Lafayette stirred awake, opening one eye and then the other. He looked to where Victoria had laid and she'd vanished. In her place there was a red rose and a folded slip of paper. Lafayette smiled seeing the flower. He picked it up and inhaled its fragrance, smiling even harder. He then laid it back down and picked up the slip of paper. He unfolded it and read over it.

Sorry, but I had to run. I had some business I needed to take care of. Last night was amazing; hopefully we can hang out again sometime soon.

Hugs and Kisses,

Vickie

At the bottom of the slip of paper there was a red lipstick imprint kiss. Lafayette folded up the slip of paper and laid it down on the dresser. He smelled the rose and looked up; his shirt that had gotten grass stains on it was hanging on the doorknob, with clear plastic draped over it; Ren had gotten it dry cleaned like he said he would. Lafayette threw the comforter off of him and slipped his slacks back on. He put on his wife-beater and slipped on the shirt that had gotten dry cleaned.

When Lafayette went down stairs he was called into the kitchen by a slender man in a chef uniform. The man spoke broken English but was very polite. He told the hustler that Ms. Couture said for him to make him anything he wanted for breakfast. Lafayette told the chef to fix him eggs, bacon, wheat toast and cheese grits.

"Yeah, and hook a nigga up with some orange juice, too." Lafayette told him.

"OK, coming right up."

"I fucks with chu. What's your name?" Lafayette dapped the chef up.

"Bizean."

"Thanks, Bizean." He patted him on his shoulder and sought solitude in the living room, where he watched television until his breakfast was done.

After Lafayette devoured his meal, he hopped into his rental and drove off the grounds of Victoria's estate. He had to get back to the hood and make sure his workers were up to open up shop and to give fiends their medicine. Though Lafayette had Gar and Lil Man to handle these dealings, he liked to keep a close eye on things himself. This was out of habit, because when it was just the three of them, he was the one making sure things were in order.

Lafayette heard the familiar chirp of a police car siren. He looked into his rearview mirror, and sure enough, there was a police cruiser behind him, colorful lights flashing. Lafayette dropped his banger on the floor between his feet. Using the heel of his shoe, he slid it underneath the driver seat and pulled over along the side of the street. He then glanced into the rearview mirror and saw the driver side door of the cruiser swing open. He placed his hands on the steering-wheel and took a deep breath, preparing himself for the confrontation. He heard the footfalls of the officer's big leather boots getting closer and closer. Before he knew it he was taping on his driver side window. Lafayette grinned and looked to the window. His facial expression changed to one of surprise when he came face to face with a smiling Montrice.

Lafayette held down the button that operated his window, making it descend down into the driver side door.

"You gotta stop doing that shit, you scared the fuck outta me, girl. You know a

nigga stay riding dirty." Lafayette informed her.

"I tried hitting you up last night but you didn't pick up. What's up with that?"

"Whoa now, pump your brakes!" Lafayette frowned. "You don't have no papers on me, and I sho' didn't put no ring on your finger. Calm that shit down."

"Well, excuse me. I was just trying to give you that information on that guy you asked about."

"Well, say that then. What chu got for me?" he flexed his fingers.

Montrice reached into her pocket and pulled out a business card. Scribbled on the back of the business card there was an address and a room number. She passed it through the window to Lafayette and he looked it over.

"That's the hospital he's in." Montrice pointed to the name of the hospital on the business card. "He's under the name Ernesto Guamo. There's one officer guarding his door."

"Cool. Good looking out." Lafayette stuck the business card into his pocket. He then looked to Montrice. She turned her cheek to him and tapped it with her finger, signaling for him to kiss her there. Lafayette leaned forth to kiss her cheek and she turned her pillow soft lips to him, causing him to kiss them. Montrice looked to him and smiled. He smiled back and shook his head.

"So, what's cracking for the night?" Montrice asked him.

"This money train, I'll hit chu up later to knock it outta the park."

"Is that so?"

"Fucking right, I'ma hit that ass like a home run in the ninth inning."

"Oooooh, I can't wait." Montrice pecked him on the lips. When she turned to walk away, he stuck his hand out of the window and smacked her on the ass. Stopping, she looked over her shoulder at him and smile, making her ass dance before continuing her stroll back to her vehicle.

Chapter 21

Lafayette pulled in front of his house and hopped out of the rental. His front yard was littered with bloods. They stood around Gar who was lying on his back pumping iron, shiny from sweat. His face was screwed up and he was clenching his teeth. His cheeks turned red as he lifted the barbell up and down from his sweaty, hairy chest. The bloods, who were either bare chest or wearing tank tops, surrounded him and encouraged him to keeping lifting. Lil Man was off to the side by his lonesome, lifting dumbbells to his shoulders, one by one. His face was a mask of concentration as he pushed his muscles to their limits, lifting iron that appeared to be half his weight. He'd been lifting for quite some time and his toned body was boasting the results. His only drawback was the more muscular he got; the shorter he seemed to appear. He didn't know it, but he was transforming into Mighty Mouse right before his peers eyes.

Lafayette stepped into the yard receiving '*What's ups?*' and head nods from the bloods, all of which he returned. He leaned his slim form against the fence and folded his arms across his chest.

"Yo, who dat?" he heard Gar ask one of the bloods.

"It's that nigga Lafayette." Said a bald headed blood wearing a red tank top. The small gold chains around his throat looked like chokers around his thick neck. His body was the exact replica of The Incredible Hulk.

"What's up?" Lil' Man approached Lafayette and gave him dap.

"Ain't shit, I just need to holla at y'all real quick."

Gar finished his last set and sat the barbell down on the weight bench's hooks. He then sat up, breathing hard as he wiped his face with a white towel. He threw the towel over his shoulder and stepped over the weight bench, heading towards Lafayette. One of the bloods took his place on the weight bench and grasped the barbell, beginning his sets.

Gar slipped off his gloves and slapped hands with his Main Man.

"What's up, La?"

"We need to chop it up." Lafayette told him. "Let's take it in the house."

Gar snatched three bottles of water out of the refrigerator; he threw Lafayette and Lil Man a bottle and sat down at the kitchen table.

"So what's on your mind, boss dawg?" Gar took a sip of water.

"I know where Garza's laying at." Lafayette held up the business card. He let it linger in the air a moment and sat it down on the table. He then slid it in front of Gar and he picked it up, looking over it.

"County General hospital; it won't take long for me to slip into his room and slip out. I'll make it quick. I'll give 'em three swift jabs to the heart. Yack! Yack! Yack!" he pretended to stab the air with an imaginary knife, three times. "Hospital staff wouldn't even know I was there." He looked from Lafayette to Lil Man, waiting for their opinion on the situation.

"That's the thing." Lafayette said.

"What's that?" Gar's forehead furrowed.

"There's a cop up there that's watching his door."

Hearing that made Gar lay back in his chair staring ahead at nothing. He took a deep breath and his shoulders slumped. He then massaged his chin and thought on it for a moment before delivering his reply. "Fuck it," he shrugged, "I'll sneak past Binem and send homie on a vacation somewhere where it's always summer. My life is money and murder."

"So you got this?" Lafayette asked. He tilted his head down and raised his eyebrows.

"Yeah, I got it." Gar said confidently.

"All right then, it's handled."

"Hold up." Lil' Man spoke up. Lafayette and Gar looked to him. They had curious expressions on their faces. "Let me get this one, Gar."

The little nigga looked him square in his eyes.

"I can handle it, Lil, don't trip." Gar assured him, tapping his fist to his chest.

"Nah, let me get down on this, I need it." Lil Man insisted, still holding eye contact. "I need to prove to myself that I'm still worth a damn…even with one eye." He pointed to his good eye. As of now he was wearing glasses with one black lens, which covered his ruined eye.

Gar blew hard and looked away from Lil Man, thinking. He eyes shifted back to Lil' Man and he said, "All right, my nigga, he's yours."

"Good looking out, Gar." Lil' Man smiled and slapped hands with him, snapping his fingers.

"Lil, you know you don't have to prove nothing to any of us." Lafayette told him. He had respect for his little homeboy, because he already knew how he gave it up in the streets. "Our whole squad knows you'll let that thang charbroil flame a nigga. There ain't no questioning that." He gripped his shoulder and looked him in the eyes.

"I know, but I'll feel better if I can go on this mission." The look in his eyes said *Please, don't take this away from me. I need this.*

"All right, I'ma give you the shoes, but chu gotta lace'em up and walk in'em." A grinning Lil Man nodded. Lafayette patted him on the back and rose from the table. The shit they had went through those past couple of months had drew the two men closer to one another. They had grown to love each other like brothers. Their bond was strong and nothing besides betrayal could break it…Nothing besides betrayal.

LATER THAT NIGHT

Lil Man stepped out of his stolen car dressed in a black policeman's uniform. The wind was blowing and the rain was hitting him hard. He adjusted his glasses and zipped up his hefty jacket. He started towards the hospital and pulled out the business card Lafayette had given him. He read over the information as he walked along. Suddenly, the business card was snatched away from his hand by a powerful wind. The business card floated across the air, with Lil Man chasing behind it. It landed on a flowing bed of water beside the curb that poured out into the gutter. The business card was just about to slip down into the gutter until Lil Man scooped it. He stood erect and looked over the card. The water had nearly washed away the information on it, leaving the ink running.

He balled up the business card and tossed it aside. Next, he headed back towards the automatic doors of the hospital, repeating the room number on the card along the way.

***

Zay was leaned back in his chair on its hind legs with his legs cross on the kitchen table. His .357 Magnum lie on the table top while he gripped the .44 Magnum revolver, spinning the chamber around. The only thing that could be heard inside of the kitchen was the chamber of the weapon being spun around consistently. Hearing La'Chat enter the kitchen, he looked up and saw her opening the refrigerator. She rummaged around inside of it until she found what she was looking for: a Heineken. After popping the cap off of the green bottle, she tossed the opener aside on the counter and approached her man, sitting down on the edge of the table.

"Sooooo, who do we have next on The Hit List, handsome?" she asked, taking a swig of her beer.

"I don't know, beautiful. Would you be so kind as to do the honors?" he picked up one of the throwing darts that was lying on the table top, extending it to her. She took it.

"With pleasure," She looked to the back wall of the kitchen and tossed the dart over in her hand. Taking a hold of it, she took aim, and threw it at the target hanging up on the wall, which was covered with photos of different drug dealers. The dart stabbed into the photo of a hustler that they were very familiar with. At that moment, Zay and La'Chat slowly turned their heads to one another, and smiles stretched across their lips.

***

Batice and Theo lay up in bed getting high together. She was in her bra and panties while he was in his boxers and socks. Theo sucked on the glass penis as he held the flame of his lighter to it. While he was indulging in his drug of choice, Batice was pushing him to hurry up so she could get a taste of the poison. Having had his blast, he allowed her to snatch the pipe and lighter from his hands. She didn't waste anytime firing up the stem and puffing up her cheeks. As she proceeded to get high, Theo lay up with his head up against the headboard. His eyes were hooded and he was scratching his bony chest. After a while, he looked to his girl and she was laid up too, holding the tools she used to smoke the drugs with. Seeing that she was out of it, he took the stem and saw that it was empty. He went to grab the Ziploc bag of crack from off of the dresser and saw that there wasn't anything left in it. Angry, he balled up the bag and threw it across the bedroom. Looking at Batice, he noticed her cleavage in her bra and her fat ass coochie imprint in her panties. A light bulb came on inside of his head and he hopped out of the bed, running to the closet. He flung open the door and went through the rack of clothes hanging up. Finding the sluttest dress that he could, he held it up to himself. He looked back and forth from the dress to Batice, imagining how she would look in it. Afterwards, he took a box down from off of the shelf inside of the closet and removed its lid, pulling out a wig. Hastily, he walked over to the bed and laid the dress upon Batice. He then sat the wig on top of her head and took a step back. Folding his arms across his chest, he tilted his head from left to right, thinking of how she'd look in what he'd laid out for her. A smile stretched across his lips and he rubbed his hands together greedily.

There was money to be made.

***

The elevator doors parted and Lil Man stepped out, still repeating the room number that was on the back of the business card to himself. Heading down the corridor he saw a police officer reading a news paper and sipping a cup of coffee. His heart quickened when he saw him, but he placed his thoughts into a killer's mind frame like he always did when he was about to get down on a hit. He no longer heard the fast pace of his heartbeat. He only saw the numbers on his prey's room door: E-296.

The police officer looked up from his news paper and took in Lil Man's appearance. He folded his news paper down and rose to his feet, looking at his watch.

"Jones, right?" the police officer asked. Lil Man nodded. "You're ten minutes early, but I'm not complaining."

"Think I can bum that paper off of ya? I forgot mine in the car."

"Sure, here you go." The police officer passed him the news paper and made his way down the corridor, whistling Dixie.

Lil Man stared down the corridor at the police officer until he made a left into the area, where all of the elevators were. He then slipped a 9 inch long, homemade shank into the fold of the news paper he was given and ducked off inside of room E-296. When he entered the room it was totally dark, but he could make out Garza lying in bed fast asleep. He smiled satanically and advanced in his intended victim's direction. When he reached the side of his bed, he pulled his shank from the fold of the news paper. He tossed the news paper aside and straddled the man he'd come to kill. He placed his hand over his prey's mouth and thrust the shank in and out of his chest, causing blood to speckle his uniform. Garza's eyes popped open and he clawed at his attacker's face. Lil Man whipped his face from left to right, trying his best to avoid his hands.

He continued to stab his victim with the homemade shank, turning his hospital gown crimson. The blood absorbed into the white sheet, turning its color as it expanded. With the last of his might, Garza reached up and grabbed his assailant by the side of his face. He pressed his thumb into his missing eye socket, causing him to howl in pain. Blood squirted in Garza's face and he pressed his thumb further into Lil Man's face. He then kneed him in the testicles and shoved him off of the bed. Lil Man hit the floor with a thud. Garza pulled the IV from out of his arm and ripped the other patches from off of his body. He rolled off the side of the bed and hit the floor. He crawled for the door, screaming for help in a hoarse voice. Holding his wounded eye, Lil Man scanned the floor until he spotted his shank. He crawled to it in a hurry and grasped it. He ran over to Garza and straddled him from behind, stabbing him in his back repeatedly with extreme prejudice. Blood went flying everywhere with each stab of his weapon.

"Die, you bitch ass nigga! Die, you mothafucka you!" Lil Man bellowed, wetting up Garza's back. His victim still kept for the door, but his movements slowed each time the shank bit into his back. He gave the fight for his life his all, but eventually his movements ceased altogether. He lay on the side of his face bugged eyed and expelled his last breath.

Lil Man breathed heavily, killing Garza was exhausting. Knives were a lot messier than guns. He could have shot him up but knives were a whole different game. You had to get up close and personal with them. There was an intimacy about them. Though the shank got the job done, this would be his last time using one. He was going to stick with what he knew best…guns.

Lil Man stood over Garza's dead body. He wiped the sweat from his forehead with the back of his bloody hand, leaving a red smear behind. Suddenly, the door swung open and he looked up. A police officer stood before him in the light that was shining on the back of him from the outside corridor, making him look like nothing more than a silhouette. He looked from the dead body up to Lil Man, drawing down on him.

"Drop the knife! Drop it, right now, goddamn it!" the police officer ordered, trigger happy as a mothafucka. This was Officer Jones. The black police officer that was supposed to take over the shift from the officer Lil Man had relieved. Lil Man dropped the shank and placed his hands behind his head. He turned his back and got down on his knees, like Officer Jones had ordered. Officer Jones checked the pulse in Garza's neck and confirmed that he was dead. He then holstered his weapon and handcuffed his suspect. He hustled him towards the door. As soon as they crossed the threshold into the corridor, Lil Man's eyes bugged and his mouth dropped open in surprise. Garza Sanchez came rolling down the hall in his direction. He was sitting in a wheelchair, being pushed along by his sister, Isabella Monroe.

When Garza had collapsed inside of the gas station that night after Lafayette had shot him, the clerk that was on duty called 911 and an ambulance rushed to the scene. He made it to the hospital in time to have his life saved. Some would have chalked it up to good luck, while others would have said it was a miracle. It didn't matter to Garza though, just as long as his brown ass was alive.

Garza looked to the dead body on the floor and then to the surprised expression on Lil Man's face. His laughing started low then it gradually grew louder and maniacal. He laughed heartily and winced from the wounds in his chest. Though it hurt him to do so, he kept on laughing as hard and as loud as he could. Lil Man looked from Garza to the dead body on the floor. It was the lifeless form was of a Mexican man that resembled Garza, but it definitely wasn't him. Lil Man hung his head and allowed Officer Jones to escort him out of the room without struggle.

As he was ushered towards the elevators doors, he could still hear Garza's haunting laughter.

"Hahahahahahahaha! Stupid mayate got the wrong fucking room! Hahahahahahaha!"

To Be Continued...

The Last Real Nigga Alive 2

AVAILABLE NOW BY TRANAY ADAMS

The Devil Wears Timbs 1-5

Bury Me A G 1-3

Tyson's Treasure 1-2

Treasure's Pain

A South Central Love Affair

Me And My Hittas 1- 6

The Last Real Nigga Alive 1-3

Fearless

COMING SOON BY TRANAY ADAMS

The Devil Wears Timbs 6: Just Like Daddy

A Hood Nigga's Blues

Billy Bad Ass

The Last Real Nigga Alive